SILVER LININGS

A HOPE HERRING MYSTERY BOOK 1

J. A. WHITING
NELL MCCARTHY

J. A. WHITING BOOKS

To hear about new books and book sales, please sign up for my mailing list at:
www.jawhiting.com

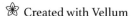 Created with Vellum

With thanks to all my readers

Dream Big

1

"When is Dad coming home?" Cori asked.

Hope looked across the kitchen to where her thirteen-year-old daughter sat at the table working on a Sudoku puzzle and waiting for the spaghetti her mother had not yet put together. The sauce was simmering, but Hope was reluctant to start boiling the noodles until she heard from her husband, Doug.

As a reporter, Doug's job sometimes took him far from Columbus. His current crusade was against a drug gang that imported and sold fentanyl. As her husband had explained, the gang had a lot of cash that they used to buy dirty local police and politicians who would look the other way.

Doug, like the bloodhound he was, had sniffed

out the corruption and chased the trail. He didn't worry much about the danger. He always shrugged it off. Most of the thugs and officials he dealt with talked a tough game, but rarely acted on their threats since going to prison for taking a bribe was nothing compared to going to prison for murder.

Hope glanced at her watch. Her husband wasn't that late, in fact, he wasn't really late at all. She'd hold off on the noodles until he called or texted because he always called or texted.

"He'll be home in a little bit," Hope told Cori. "He's working."

"He's always working." Cori frowned. "He's supposed to help me with my science project."

"I can help you with it," Hope offered.

"Like you did last year?" Cori giggled. "It exploded, remember?"

Hope did remember. The explosion was spectacular, only it wasn't supposed to happen. She didn't want to take credit for the explosion, but it really was her fault. Of course, that was the chance Cori took when she asked her mother, the social studies teacher, to help on a science project.

"That was a simple mistake of adding too much baking soda." The corners of Hope's mouth turned up. "I misread the instructions."

"And that's why I'll wait for Dad," Cori said with a big grin.

Hope couldn't fault her daughter's logic. Why trust mom, when dad was a seriously better scientist?

"Would you watch the sauce pot?" Hope asked. "It's simmering. Turn it down if it starts to sputter."

"All right." Cori was working on a math problem.

"I'm going to grade some tests in my office. When Dad gets home, come get me."

"Yep."

Hope retreated to her first-floor office, which used to be a den. Doug's office was on the second floor in the small bedroom. They knew it was better that they didn't share a space.

Hope's office smelled of lilac and featured two large windows that let in the sunlight, even in the dead of winter. Doug had put a large white board partially over his window, sending the room into near twilight, even on bright days. Her shelves were filled with neatly arranged books and binders. His shelves were stuffed with manuscripts and half-read books, in no particular order. Her desk featured a docking station, so she could use her laptop wherever she was in the house. Doug's old, steel desk held up an old-fashioned desktop computer. He had a laptop, but only used it when he was out. He was always transferring files via Internet or flash drive. Hope knew that she could never work in a space filled with Doug's lack of organization so separate offices were the solution.

Hope didn't bother sitting at the desk. She pulled her shoulder-length brown hair into a messy bun, then plopped into the overstuffed chair, her folder of tests on the table next to her. She opened the file and took out the first answer sheet with the name Brady Schnurr written on the top of the paper.

Brady wasn't the smartest boy in the class, but he wasn't the least capable either. Hope guessed Brady would score somewhere in the 80s, right on the cusp between a 'B' and a 'C.' Since this wasn't an essay test, Hope couldn't fudge in any direction. The number spoke for itself. The test took less than five minutes to grade. She wrote 87 at the top and added a little note—*well done*. Brady and his parents would be satisfied with the grade. The young man was a solid middle-of-the-class student.

Hope worked through the tests expecting at any moment to be summoned to the kitchen. At five minutes per test, she could correct the entire class in less than two hours. If she skipped some personal notes, she could finish even faster, but she liked to add positive comments. A bit of encouragement or a frank assessment of a problem might be all a student needed to do better. She didn't have to finish grading all of the tests because her first period the next day was a planning period. She could finish the grading then if she needed to.

Hope had graded a dozen tests before she decided to see if Doug had arrived home. She checked her phone, but there was still no message from him.

A flicker of worry ran through her body. It was odd that Doug hadn't contacted her.

She went into the kitchen where Cori was busy with her tablet computer. Lots of the kids had tablets since they were simple to use and easy to carry.

"Did your father text you?" Hope asked.

"Nope," Cori answered as she absent-mindedly twisted a strand of her long brown hair.

Hope looked at the clock. "Well, too bad for him. I'm hungry. We're eating dinner."

"It's about time," Cori agreed. "I'm starving."

"Would you set the table for us?" Hope asked.

"For two or three?"

"Three, but you know what is going to happen," Hope said with a smile. "Once we get all the work done, he'll come through the door."

"He's good at that," Cori said shaking her head.

"Very good."

It was fifteen minutes before Hope sat down with a plate of spaghetti and a salad. Cori dove into the salad while looking at her tablet.

"Ahem," Hope said. "Tablet."

Cori looked up, and Hope shook her head.

With a little groan, Cori put aside the tablet and kept eating.

Hope said. "This is our dinner hour, our time to chat."

"Why do you always want to chat?" Cori asked lifting a forkful of salad from her plate.

"Because dinner talk is fast becoming a lost art. People don't take the time and effort to engage with each other. Now, it's just wolf down your food while staring at your phone or computer screen. People aren't robots. We need to interact, and dinner is the perfect time to talk about our days. Tell me what you learned in school today."

Cori frowned. "Do I have to?"

"No, we can talk about your last math test, if you'd rather do that."

"Am I still paying for that? Don't you forget anything?"

"What did you learn in school today?" Hope

tried to get some chat going.

"I learned that climate change is happening fast and we only have a few years to change things. The climate is always changing, and it's been warmer than in the past, and colder, too."

They talked about ways that could slow climate change and then Hope asked, "What else did you learn?"

Hope liked to talk to her daughter about her day in school. Not only did Cori learn polite dinner chat, but the talking kept Cori from scarfing down her food and running off to her room. Slowing down the dinner process was a good thing, in Hope's opinion. Cori was getting older and, too often, they were finished in ten minutes and that was hardly any time to connect with each other.

As they talked, Hope kept looking at the clock and to the back door. The clock told her Doug was very late. The back door should have opened by now. Doug should be smiling at them and recounting some funny anecdote about a farmer around Dayton or a pawn shop operator in Cleveland. Doug was a very good storyteller and Hope and Cori loved to hear his tales. Hope wished he was right there in the kitchen with them making them laugh.

2

Although the clock moved, the door stayed closed. They finished dinner and clean-up, and Cori retreated to the living room to finish her homework. Hope fixed a plate for Doug and slid it into the fridge, and then she went back to her office to finish grading the tests. After that, she'd lay out her clothes for the next day. Hope had a tidy streak in her. Doug, on the other hand, wasn't as neat, although, his work files were impeccable. He tracked everything about a story, writing out copious notes. She always wondered how he could be so detail-oriented about one thing and not another.

By the time Hope had laid out her outfit for the next day and packed up her briefcase, she'd started to worry. It wasn't that Doug couldn't get waylaid by a breaking story. That happened once in a while.

What bothered her was that he hadn't checked in with her. That was unusual, very unusual, so she did what she rarely ever did when he was working. She called him.

And was greeted by his voicemail.

"All right," Hope said trying to keep the worry out of her voice. "You're late, so please call and let us know what's up. Let me know you're okay. Love you." When she clicked off the phone, alarm bells rang in her head.

Hope really started to worry when it was time for Cori to go to bed, but she tried hard to push away her feelings of unease. When Doug did arrive, he would have a perfectly legitimate explanation. It was always like that. Hope tried to convince herself she was worrying for nothing.

"Where's Dad?" Cori asked as she hugged her mother goodnight.

"Out doing his job," Hope said.

"But he always calls," Cori said. "He didn't call tonight."

"He *almost* always calls, and I'm sure he has a good reason why he hasn't."

"Like what?"

"He lost his phone, or his phone ran out of power, or he's stuck some place where he can't get a signal, or there's a breaking story. There are lots of reasons why he can't call us."

"You don't think something bad happened to him, do you?" Cori's voice held a tinge of worry.

"No, no, nothing bad, nothing bad at all. It's just one of those things. You know, like when you forget to take your phone to school."

"I only did that twice."

"And both times, you needed to make a call and couldn't."

"Okay, I get it."

Hope kissed her daughter on the forehead. "Dad will be home soon, and he'll kiss you good night when he gets in."

"Promise?"

"Promise. Now, go have a good sleep."

"Good night, Mom."

Hope turned off the light and closed the door. She was pretty sure Cori wouldn't go right to sleep. Her daughter worried at times, especially about her father. Hope wondered just when that had started. She couldn't pinpoint an exact day, but it might have been when Doug spent three weeks in Boston, investigating a city councilman whose business partner and wife were found murdered. While Doug had called home every day, his absence made Cori anxious. Well, Hope had to admit that his absence made her anxious too, and maybe, her worry had bled over to Cori.

Hope locked the doors and grabbed a book from the bookcase, a mystery, which was her favorite kind of story. She liked to think she would have been a good detective. She had that sort of mind. Means, motive, and opportunity. Red herrings. The citizen detective, all the tropes of the genre. She liked stretching her brain to solve the murder and she was a very good researcher. Once in a while, she got fooled when reading a story, but she had learned the steps of the plots, the gradual build, the unexpected witness. She would have made a very good law enforcement officer.

She settled into her chair and opened the book. While a small voice nagged at her, reminding her that Doug hadn't called, she pushed the voice to the side. She would read until it was her bedtime. The last thing she was going to do was worry herself sick. She had to keep her mind busy so she wouldn't dwell on what might be wrong.

Hope had only read a few pages when outside lights splashed across the wall, the red and blue lights of some sort of emergency vehicle. With her heart hammering, she went to the window and looked out. A state police cruiser was in their driveway, the lights flashing.

Hope put her hand against the wall and bit her lip as her vision seemed to swim.

When the doorbell rang, she could barely take a breath.

Hope hurried to the front door. She looked through the peep hole at the state trooper, his Mountie hat on his head, and with tears gathering in the corner of her eyes, she opened the door hoping the officer was at the wrong house.

A serious-faced man looked at her.

"Who is it?" Cori asked.

Hope turned around. Her daughter stood behind her.

Hope said, "It's a policeman."

"Oh, no. Oh, no." Cori gripped onto her mother's arm.

With gathering dread, Hope looked back at the trooper.

"Hope Herring?" the trooper asked.

"Yes," she answered, her voice barely above a whisper.

"May I come in for a moment, Ma'am?"

"Oh, yes, sorry. I ... I don't know...."

She opened the door wider and stepped back to let the officer in, and after that, she didn't remember much of anything.

3

Hope watched as the last of her household goods were loaded into the moving van. Cori was already in the backseat of the SUV, the back of which was stuffed with the things Hope didn't trust to the movers. Mostly, it was her computers and jewelry and a TV, and photos she didn't want to lose. She had heard too many stories of moving vans disappearing or rolling off a mountain or catching on fire. She had insurance, but insurance would only replace the type of thing that was lost, not the thing itself. Anything that she couldn't bear to lose was in her Toyota Highlander.

The van driver locked up the doors and climbed behind the wheel of the van. Hope watched as it pulled away from the house, the house where she'd lived for the last fifteen years, the house she no longer owned. At the age of forty-two, she had to remake her life.

For one last time, she looked at the place that had been their home. Fifteen years of memories had been made inside that house. She had to keep reminding herself that the memories were inside her head ... not left inside the house. Her memories would travel with her. They wouldn't be left behind.

Doug would be with her wherever she went. He would always be in her heart. Hope's throat tightened with emotion. *Doug.*

A house was just wood and brick. She and Cori would make a home in their next house.

With a sad smile, Hope climbed into her SUV. "Ready?" she asked her daughter.

"I wish we weren't moving," Cori said.

"I know," Hope said. "But we need to move."

"Why? I like it here. My friends are here. Dad is here."

"I promise we'll come back and visit him."

"That's not the same. Who'll take care of him?" Cori looked wistfully out the car window.

"The cemetery will take care of it."

"Not like we would." The teenager pouted.

"We'll come back. I promise."

"When?"

"When it's time."

"That's like saying never."

Hope put the vehicle in gear. "No, it's saying what it's saying. Try not to think about what you're leaving behind. Think about the possibilities ahead."

"Why do you hate me?"

"I love you, and you know it."

"If you loved me, you wouldn't take me to a new state. You'd let us stay here."

"It's North Carolina, and I'm taking you there because I do love you. It's a new start for us."

"I don't want a new start. I want my old house and my old friends."

"Sometimes, it's better to get a clean start. And it's warmer in North Carolina."

"And buggier. I checked."

"We won't be far from the ocean," Hope forced her voice to sound optimistic.

"I don't need the ocean."

Hope knew that no matter what she said, Cori would find a way to argue about it. Yet, Hope didn't want to just end the talk.

"How about a deal?" Hope said. "Two years."

"Two years? That's, like, forever."

"It's not 'like' anything. Two years. Let's give it

two years, and if you're still unhappy, we'll give it two more years."

"Ha, ha," Cori deadpanned.

"No, really, if you're still unhappy after two years, we'll look for another place."

"But not back here?"

"No, I don't think we'll come back here."

"That's not much of a deal."

"It's the best I can do right now."

"I'll take it, but I don't have to like it."

"We can either embrace the change or fight it, but embracing it will make us happier."

"Hah."

Hope glanced at the rearview mirror. Cori was tapping on her tablet computer. That was the signal to stop chatting and just drive. She had a good six hours on the road before they stopped in West Virginia. With any luck, Cori would sleep for some of those hours. Luckily, the sun was shining and the roads were clear. There might be a storm ahead, but Hope knew it wouldn't be weather-related. She had to stifle a sigh of sadness.

As she drove, Hope asked herself for the thousandth time if she was doing the right thing. Cori was right. They were leaving behind friends and home and Doug's...grave. But without him, the house had become something other than a home. It was a reminder of what had been, what could never be again. She wasn't willing to live in the past, in what had been. She wouldn't ever forget the past, the happy times, but she couldn't live there anymore. If she stayed, she would still be living in a past that was lost to her. Even without good answers, she still needed to move on—at least for now.

North Carolina was far enough away for a new start.

Hope got the silent treatment for the rest of the day. Cori remained in the bubble created by her tablet computer. Even through lunch, Cori limited herself to monosyllabic answers.

Hope didn't push. Cori's anger and fear would work out in time. Dinner was a little better as they'd checked in to their hotel room, something Cori found new and exciting. Hope played up the newness, the change. They were on their way to a new life. That was exciting, wasn't it? Things were looking up until bedtime.

When the lights went out, fear and uncertainty came with the darkness. Hope could hear Cori sniffling, fighting the tears that came with their terrible loss.

Hope second-guessed herself. *Was* she doing the

right thing? A child's tears were powerful things. Guilt was a monkey who perched on a shoulder and chattered incessantly.

She was doing what they needed to do. They had to move on.

Breakfast wasn't a gabfest as Hope had her own doubts. After they'd eaten, they climbed into the Highlander for another six hours. Again, a bright day, an easy drive, another six hours farther from before.

Hope concentrated on the driving. Occasionally, she spotted Cori staring out the window. The scenery had changed. Tall pine trees had replaced the large canopies of the Midwest. Strange city names—Turkey, Chingaquin, Top Sail, Burgaw, Fuquay-Varina—appeared on the highway signs. Hope knew that in time, she and Cori would count the names as normal and right.

In time.

At last, Hope pulled the Highlander into the driveway of their new-old house. It was a two-story-plus attic behemoth not far from the town square. At a hundred-plus years old, it was a house that had been through any number of storms, floods, and hurricanes. Hope knew what a hurricane was, but she had never been through one. With a wish that things here would be good, she let her eyes roam over the new place.

Cori climbed out and stood by her mother.

"It looks spooky," Cori said.

"I guess it does, doesn't it? I suppose most old houses look spooky. But with some paint and new landscaping, it will look as good as, well, as good as a beautiful antique house."

Cori almost laughed, which was a good sign. Hope could work with an almost laugh.

"Come on. Let's take a look before we unload. No better time than when the rooms are empty."

Hope had received the keys when she closed on the house, so she unlocked the front door and led Cori inside. The first thing they both noticed was the smell. The house smelled as if it hadn't been aired out in decades … perhaps, it hadn't.

"This doesn't smell good," Cori said, her mouth turning down in a frown.

"That's why we're going to open the windows," Hope answered. "The fresh air will take care of the smell."

The layout of the house was decidedly former century. There was a central hall that ran straight back to the kitchen. To one side was a parlor that was small and plain, but featured a working fireplace. She thought the room would make a nice office, although there were no bookshelves. But she could have that fixed.

"What was this room?" Cori asked.

"A parlor," Hope answered.

"What's a parlor?"

"It's like a living room where people entertained their guests. You can look it up and find out more information."

"Why do you always say that? Look it up."

"Because if you look it up, you're more likely to remember the definition. Science."

"Hah." Cori shook her head.

The room across the hall from the parlor seemed to be a living room. It was small, too, and it didn't have a fireplace like the parlor did. There were book-shelves, but they didn't look to be original, probably added by one of the many owners who had lived in the house over the years.

"Another parlor?" Cori asked.

"A living room," Hope answered.

"Looks like a library."

Hope considered the room for a moment. "You may be right. Would you like to use this as your office?"

"I don't need an office."

"Well, you could make it a study room. A place where you can do your homework."

"TV room," Cori said with a smile. "Big screen TV and game console."

Hope laughed. "Okay, probably."

The next room was the dining room and it featured a chandelier and large windows. Hope knew her dining room set would fit nicely in the space. It would be fun to host dinners in the room ... eventually. For now, Hope was more than happy to be a hermit of sorts.

"This is really nice." Cori pointed to the wainscoting.

"It is. This house has beautiful wood trim and finishes."

Across from the dining room was a rather large half-bath. To Hope's eye, it was obviously an add-on with modern fixtures, but it worked for her. The hall ended in the large kitchen. The built-in appliances were newish, but not state of the art. There was room for a table and chairs where she supposed they would eat most of their meals. The pantry was more than big enough and beyond the kitchen was the mud-laundry room and the door to the backyard. Hope and Cori stepped out the door and examined the yard.

"Pretty small," Cori said.

"You might not think so when you're mowing it."

"*I'm* going to mow it?"

"There are only the two of us and the chores have to be done. So, yes, I think you might be the one to mow it."

"And trim all those bushes?" Cori's face had an expression of horror.

The backyard was a tangle of bushes. Hope thought they were honeysuckle, but she wasn't sure.

"Sooner or later, but that's a fall job, not a summer one."

"That's good."

A weathered, wooden fence ran along the sides of the yard, cutting off the view of neighboring houses, which weren't all that close. Having some neighbors nearby made Hope feel safe.

"How about a pool?" Cori asked. "A pool would cut down on the mowing and give us a place to cool off."

"Maybe someday," Hope said. "For now, we have to watch our spending." She knew things were going to be tight, now that Doug was gone. Her heart ached.

The second floor showed more renovation. The master bedroom had been created by combining two smaller bedrooms. The bathroom had been added, and it was a nice, modern one. The other two bedrooms were good sized and bright. Cori picked the bigger one, which was fine with Hope. That room was closer to the other upstairs bathroom. The last bedroom would be the guest bedroom—if they ever had an overnight guest. That brought them to the narrow door at the end of the hall.

"What's this?" Cori asked.

"I don't know," Hope answered. "I don't remember it in the quick online run-through I had. Let's go see."

4

The door opened to a steep, narrow staircase that led to another narrow door. Hope opened the door and entered an attic. The attic was much like any attic, with the exception of the wall at one end, with its own door. Cori beat Hope to the door and opened it into a medium-sized room.

"What is this?" Cori asked.

"I don't know," Hope answered. "But it has a nice view of the courthouse. I suppose it could have been a sewing room or something. Maybe an art studio for painting. That makes sense. It has really good light and a nice view."

"Painting?" Cori asked. "No one does that anymore."

"Sure, they do. It's a nice space. I think I'll make this my office," Hope said. "I think I can be very productive up here."

"You mean, you can hide up here," Cori said.

"I don't hide."

"Hah."

Cori led the way back down to the kitchen. Hope followed, suddenly feeling pleased with the discovery of the studio in the attic. She didn't know much about the previous occupants, but she supposed they had left part of themselves throughout the house. She and Cori would leave their mark, too.

In the kitchen, they started opening windows, which didn't prove to be an easy task. The old, double-hung windows hadn't been opened in a while, and they were stiff and stuck. Half the windows couldn't be opened at all, which bothered Hope. She should have done a better inspection before she bought the house. Now, she would need to hire a handyman to fix the windows.

"Is there a basement?" Cori asked as they opened windows.

"No," Hope answered. "This is what they call 'low country,' and the water table is high. Basements flood very easily around here so, they build every-thing with a crawl space."

"I think I'd like a basement."

Hope chuckled. "Then you'll have to start digging."

Cori laughed.

The second floor windows proved to be no easier to open than the ones on the ground floor, and again, half the windows wouldn't budge. Hope supposed that the uncooperative windows were an added security feature. No burglar would ever get through them.

Hope decided to go up to the attic to open the windows in the studio. As she entered the room, she felt a sudden chill, which seemed impossible. The room was on the HVAC system, so it could be heated and cooled, but this chill was nothing like air conditioning.

As Hope struggled with a window, she had the unnerving feeling that someone was watching her, staring at her. The feeling was so intense that she spun from the window to see who was in the room.

She was alone.

For a moment, she just stared, looking all around the space. Then, she chided herself. What did she expect in a new house? Of course, she was going to get strange feelings from time to time, especially when she was alone. In fact, she knew that she was going to hear strange sounds, too. No two houses were the same, and yet, all houses came equipped with their own bunch of creaks and groans. When those happened, she was not going to act like a frightened schoolgirl. She had to expect new sounds that she wasn't used to.

After finally opening the window, Hope still had the unnerving sensation that someone was watching her and it was hard to shake the feeling.

She left all the doors open so that the attic window would act as a natural vent, with the hot air rising and passing outside through the window. She hoped the bad smell would go away with the air. A nice honeysuckle scent would be welcome.

As she descended to the ground floor, she wondered when the furniture would arrive. The answer to her text told her that the moving van wouldn't arrive until the next day. That meant a comfortable and costly night in a motel, or an uncomfortable night sleeping on the floor in the house. She decided that over lunch, she would let Cori decide which choice would be best.

"Let's stay in the house," Cori said as she bit into her hamburger.

"Are you sure? We'll have to sleep on the floor on blow-up mattresses."

"We can do it. No, wait, are the lights working? I forgot about that."

"The utilities are on, but we don't have any of our stuff. No sheets or towels or anything."

"Maybe, it's not such a good idea then. I guess we should go to a motel."

"Yeah," Hope said. "We'll unload the SUV and find a room for the night. Sound good?"

"It does," Cori answered. "I forgot that we don't even have wi-fi yet."

Hope chuckled. She knew that for the younger generation, wi-fi was as important as food, probably even more important.

They managed to unload the SUV, placing the items in the rooms where they would end up. Then, they went about closing the windows which was as difficult as opening them had been. Still, the house did smell better. When Hope traipsed up the attic stairs, she discovered the door to her "new" office was closed.

That struck her as odd, but she supposed the draft had been strong enough to shut the door. As she locked the window, she experienced the same feeling as before.

Someone was watching her. She could feel someone's eyes. Giving herself a shake, she told herself she was being silly. She and Cori had examined every room in the empty house. No one could be hiding. She would have to get over the weird feeling.

While Cori stared at her tablet in the motel room, Hope did a quick review of her financial status. While she thought she had enough for all of the upcoming expenses, she knew things would be tight. She needed a job before the fall term started at the middle school where she would teach. She opened her laptop to hunt for jobs in and around Castle Park, their new home. She was pretty sure no one needed a social studies teacher in the summer, but she had other skills. She was especially enthusiastic about a job she spotted for a baker and cake maker. All she had to do was apply in person at the Butter Up Bakery in town.

Hope was an accomplished baker and could produce all kinds of desserts and baked goods. While the job probably wouldn't pay great, it wouldn't be full time work either. That was good enough for her. Just enough extra money to get them past the summer months, and if it paid a little more than that, it would be even better.

Before she fell asleep that night, Hope thought

again about the feeling she had in the attic studio of someone watching her, and an icy chill ran down her spine. Was it really a good idea to turn the room into her office? Before she could answer the question, she fell fast asleep.

5

_____

"Where do you want the desk?" the mover asked early the next morning.

"In the attic," Hope said. "Please be careful though, it will be a tight fit."

"We'll get it up there, lady. Don't worry."

Hope watched as the two movers grabbed the bubble-wrapped desk and started for the stairs. The desk wasn't huge and it wasn't terribly heavy, but it would be an awkward thing to carry up the narrow steps leading to the attic.

"I want it to face the windows, if you could," Hope added.

"You got it."

Hope immediately questioned her decision as she hadn't yet checked if there was an outlet nearby to power her computer or a connection to the cable system. She knew she could use a router for the wi-fi, but would her router be strong enough? She might need some kind of pod system with boosters throughout the house. It was a detail she hadn't yet addressed, not that the problem wasn't solvable. It was just another unseen expense, another reason to contact the Butter Up Bakery as soon as possible.

Hope sighed. Money. It was the bane of most people's existence. The days when there was more than enough were rare. Still, she had enough ... for now. It was that precipitous edge that she feared. Living on a thin line was not comforting in the least.

"Can I go outside?" Cori asked.

"Sure, stay in the yard though," Hope answered.

"I need to use my phone as a hotspot," Cori said. "Is that okay?"

Hope thought a moment. "Yes, but you'll drain your battery faster."

"I know," Cori said as she headed for the back door.

"In an hour or so," Hope said, "I'll need your help setting up the kitchen."

"Call me when you're ready." Cori headed outside.

Hope knew the hard work of unpacking would

take days, if not weeks. She guessed that some items might never be unpacked, remaining in boxes in the attic. That was the way of moves. And those unopened boxes should be tossed if they hadn't been opened in a year. Didn't she read that somewhere? If you didn't open the box, then you didn't need the contents. It was good advice.

With a cup, a spoon, and some instant coffee, Hope used the microwave to make a cup of coffee. The movers would be a while, especially since they were on the hook to put the beds together and load on the box springs and mattresses.

She carried the cup around and answered the questions thrown at her by the movers. The furniture was placed precisely, and the pictures were leaned against the walls where they would someday hang. With every passing minute, Hope recognized a task that had to be done sooner or later. Some things could wait.

It was mid-afternoon before the movers were finished. She gave them extra money for food and drink and thanked them for their help. Then, she looked about her house and her shoulders drooped. She saw a mountain of work and wondered if she had the stamina to do all she needed to do. Since Doug died, Hope sometimes ran out of energy as her body flooded with the fatigue of grief.

She walked down the hall and out into the yard to find Cori sitting in an old lawn chair staring at her phone. There was a warm breeze and the scent of flowers on the air.

"This will be nice when we can get some chairs and a table to sit at under the trees," Hope said.

"Yeah. It's nice out here," Cori agreed.

"Shall we get started on setting up the kitchen?"

"I'm ready." Cori stood and put her phone in her pocket. "Let's do it."

Inside, Hope pointed to the box labeled *sink*. "The things in that box go under the sink."

Cori frowned. "Shouldn't we just buy new stuff?"

"Nope, the stuff we brought with us is perfectly good. Let's get to work."

Cori walked slowly across the room. "Maybe we should eat first."

"Work first, eat later. It's always a good motto."

"Hah."

Hope watched as her daughter sank to her knees on the hardwood floor and opened the cabinet doors.

Cori let out a groan of horror and backed away.

With wide eyes, Hope asked, "What is it?"

"There's a mouse, a dead mouse." Cori frowned.

"Throw it in the trash."

"I'm not touching it."

"Not with your hands. Use a paper towel or something. Better yet, get the broom and dustpan and sweep it up."

"It's so icky."

"What do you mean icky?"

Hope walked over and looked under the sink. The mouse in question was small, very small, and its eyes bulged out of its head. It did indeed look icky, but it was no doubt dead.

"It's just been dead for a while," Hope said. "And its skin is shrinking. That's all."

Hope didn't know if that was true, but it made sense. She knew that humans were the same way. When the dead skin shrank, the nails and hair seemed to grow. In the middle ages, people who dug up graves were of the opinion that the person had been buried alive.

While Cori fetched the broom and dustpan, Hope examined the cabinet. The last thing she needed was a nest of baby mice or a bunch of mouse droppings, but there wasn't anything in there. Which she thought was odd. She should have found something that the mouse left behind.

It was almost as if the mouse had been placed there for some reason. But that couldn't be. Why would anyone leave a dead mouse under the sink?

It was just an unlucky mouse who happened to die in the cabinet. Then, Hope considered the possibility that maybe there was some sort of poison in the house. Someone might have put poison in the crawl space or in the attic or in a closet. She would have to search that out.

After the dead mouse episode passed, the stocking of the kitchen proceeded. Cutlery and everyday dishes were unpacked and stacked in the cabinets and the pantry was filled with the few food items they'd brought along. It took several hours, but by the end, the small appliances were on the countertops and plugged into wall sockets. The containers for sugar, flour, and other staples lined the wall. The kitchen looked like a kitchen. It looked good.

"Ready for a break?" Hope asked.

"Yes, I am," Cori answered. "And I know how the mouse got in there."

"So, do I," Hope said. "It came up the wall and around the drain pipe."

"Nope. It was a cat."

"A cat?" Hope's face had a puzzled expression. "Have you seen a cat in the house?"

"No, but it makes sense. Cats are always killing mice and birds, and they don't always eat them. Sometimes, they just leave them places."

"It must have been a very clever cat," Hope said. "It got inside the house somehow. It had to either find a mouse inside the house or it brought one in. And it had to get the cabinet door open, so it could drop the mouse for you to find."

Cori frowned. "You always take the fun out of things."

"I'm just pointing out Occam's Razor."

"Is that some kind of a new shaver?" Cori looked confused.

"In the past, a razor was a proposition, something that was true without proof."

"Sort of a like a theorem? We learned about theorems in math."

"Yes, a theory. Occam was a thinker, and he came up with the razor that said when you have many different theories to explain something, the simplest theory is generally correct."

"The mouse sneaking in by itself is simpler than a clever cat?"

"It would seem that way."

"But Occam wasn't always right, was he?" Cori asked.

"No, sometimes the complicated answer is correct, but the lesson is not to make things more complicated than they need to be."

"Okay, great. Let's eat."

Hope laughed. "Now, that's simple."

Hope ordered delivery for a pizza with pepperoni and mushrooms because it felt like too much work to go out and get one. They ate in the kitchen, trading barbs about the new-old house and the dead mouse. For Hope, it was fun to joust with her daughter. At least, Cori wasn't depressed and not talking. It seemed as if her daughter was starting to embrace her new surroundings.

Despite Occam's razor, Cori was still holding out for a very clever cat.

After dinner, they fixed up their beds. While they might be able to put off some of the other housemaking tasks, they needed beds. While they had a little more time to do another job or two before bedtime, Hope decided enough was enough.

They set up the TV in the living room and battled the cable hookup for an hour. Hope considered that while electronics had made life easier, the engineers behind the devices had yet to devise a foolproof setup procedure. What was intuitive to an engineer was a mystery to an under-educated user. She and Cori finally managed to connect the TV and watch two shows before they realized they couldn't keep their eyes open and that sleep was the best option. The next day would be a non-stop effort to put the house into a livable condition.

It was while Hope was slipping on her pajamas that she felt someone was watching her. She looked for some kind of camera, hidden somewhere in the master bedroom. She uncovered nothing, but that didn't make her feel any better. She knew, just knew someone was watching.

Hope told herself she was being paranoid, but she just couldn't shake the feeling that someone was nearby. It was crazy, but it was true. Lying in bed, staring at a strange ceiling and a light that didn't work, Hope wondered when this strange, new feeling would subside. She missed their old house. She missed Doug so much.

Sleep drifted over her, and she dozed in between sleep and wakefulness.

That was when she heard the sound of footsteps.

She bolted upright.

Hope looked around in the dark, fully expecting to find someone standing next to the bed, because the sounds hadn't come from outside the room. Someone had to be close, very close. Cold sweat dribbled down her back.

She looked all around. She couldn't see well in the dark, but she could tell there was no one in her room. She was all alone, and that made her shiver.

Because she didn't *feel* all alone.

Was someone there with her?

A small voice inside her head told her that she was making up things, hearing sounds that couldn't be. She was alone, all alone. Cori was down the hall, no doubt asleep by now. There couldn't be anyone in the bedroom with her. It was impossible. Tears gathered in Hope's eyes, but she blinked them away. Over the past months, she'd cried until she didn't think she could cry anymore.

She settled back into the bed, but she didn't close her eyes. She listened. She listened for a footstep or a rustle or something that would pinpoint an intruder.

The voice inside her head told her there was no intruder, but that voice wasn't always right. Hope knew what she heard. It sounded just like someone was in her room.

After an hour, she fell asleep, still wondering if she was all alone.

The morning light woke her, and the first thing she did was look around the room. Despite seeing no one, the feeling of being watched couldn't be shaken. Hope knew it was anxiety over their move that was causing her feelings of distress.

She slipped out of bed and dressed. Her shower would have to wait until she had a chance to unpack the towels and soaps and shampoos. That task was high on the list. But first things came first ... breakfast and coffee ... not necessarily in that order.

Hope was on her second cup of coffee and more than halfway to decking out the downstairs half-bath, when Cori knocked on the door frame.

"Hey," Cori said.

"There's milk in the fridge and cereal on the table," Hope said. "Help yourself."

"I will, but who's the guy in the hall?"

Hope's blood froze in her veins. "What guy in what hall?"

"The guy in the hall upstairs. He was faced the other way, so I didn't see him very well. As soon as I said 'hello,' he zipped down the stairs. So, who is he?"

"There isn't anyone in the house except me and you," Hope said trying very hard to keep her tone of voice even and calm. "Are you sure you saw something? Maybe it was a shadow or the light changing from a passing cloud."

"I don't usually see people who aren't there, Mom, but I guess it could have been a shadow."

"I haven't seen anyone," Hope said, "and I haven't heard anyone either." She wasn't counting the sounds in the bedroom.

"Maybe it was just me, but I thought I saw someone."

"Have some breakfast, then you can outfit your bathroom with all your stuff."

"Aye, aye, captain." Cori saluted her mother.

Hope watched her daughter head for the kitchen and thought about the footsteps from last night ... and that unnerving feeling of being watched. While the feeling wasn't so strong now, it was still there, like a buzz in the background, like something that couldn't be pinned down. She was pretty sure Cori had not seen a man in the hall, but what was it that Cori *had* seen? A mix of sun and shadow? The projection of a young girl's imagination?

Hope shook herself. It was only the newness of the house. It was just the feeling of everything being unsettled. She had things to do, starting with her bathroom.

It was after the towels and sheets were put

away and the cabinets stocked that Hope took the time to get herself another cup of coffee. She passed Cori who was busy in her bathroom, standing on a stool and hanging the shower curtain. Hope might have offered some advice, but Cori's ears were stuffed with buds, so there was no use.

Hope sipped her coffee and looked out the window. The next house was several lots away, giving her the feeling of being more alone than she was. She didn't see how the "being watched" feeling could come from a nosy neighbor. Everyone was too far away. Shaking her head, she headed for her bedroom. It was the next chore on her list.

At noon, Hope took Cori to a burger place for lunch knowing that eating inside the house would only make them aware of all the work yet to be done. It was better to get away from the stuff still gnawing at her sense of home. As long as there were boxes waiting to be unpacked, they wouldn't feel free to do other things.

"How do you like the house so far?" Hope asked.

"It's okay," Cori answered. "Do you like it?"

"Yeah, so far. Let's see if we can get the wi-fi working so you can send some pictures to your friends."

"I was thinking. Can I invite some of my old friends to visit?"

"That would be fine. Just as soon as we get the house in order. I don't want to entertain while it needs basic work."

Cori grinned. "We'll get it done in no time. I'm going to invite Zoe."

"Works for me." Hope liked Zoe. The teenager was polite, friendly, and fun, and Zoe's parents were part of the small contingent that didn't ask a million questions about Doug's death.

Back at the house, Hope had only the slightest problem with the cable modem. Adding the router was straightforward. They tested the setup, and Cori had good reception in her bedroom and thankfully, Hope experienced the same success. Then, while Cori was busy taking and sending pics, Hope climbed to the attic room to set up her computer and test the wi-fi up there.

The computer started as soon as she turned it on. That was good. But it would not connect to the wi-fi, which was not good. In fact, neither Hope's tablet, nor her phone would connect to the wi-fi. That meant she would need some boosters inside the house. She couldn't work if she couldn't access the internet. It was while she was connecting the external drive that the message appeared on the computer screen. It wasn't the standard, operating system message. It was in large red letters on the screen....

LDP

6

The letters on the screen meant nothing to Hope, and after a few seconds, they disappeared. She didn't even need to tap the keyboard. She stared at the screen, wondering what had prompted the message. She wasn't connected to the internet so it couldn't have come from outside the house. In fact, she wasn't connected to any network. And the message wasn't anything like the standard error messages she was familiar with.

For a moment, she wondered if the message had been there at all. No, she was certain it had been there. But what did it mean?

By dinner time, the house had taken on the faint feeling of a home. There were still boxes to be unpacked, but the essential areas had been put together. Hope was feeling pretty good about her decision to move to Castle Park. While the neighbors hadn't beaten a path to her door to deliver any welcomes, Hope wasn't disappointed. She wasn't ready to invite people into the house anyway.

"We're done for the day," Hope told Cori over a meal of hotdogs and mac-n-cheese.

"Yay," Cori said. "Can I watch TV?"

"Sure thing, and chat with your friends."

"They like the house. They think it's cool. Zoe asked if it was haunted."

"What did you tell her?"

"That it is." Cori laughed. "Zoe believes everything you tell her, and she hates haunted houses. She doesn't even like Halloween. Well, she likes the candy."

"Who doesn't like candy. But if you want her to visit someday, you might want to tell her that the house isn't haunted at all."

"I will eventually, but it's fun to scare Zoe. She gets really excited when you do that."

"By the way," Hope said. "Do you know what the computer message LDP means?"

Cori shook her head. "I've never heard of it. Some kind of error message?"

"I think so, but since I don't have any internet connection, I can't search the net for the meaning."

"But your computer is working?"

"Perfectly. But you know computers, you ignore an error message and pretty soon, you get the blue screen of death."

Cori laughed. "I know. I'll look it up, if you want."

"Great. That would help ... I hope."

Cori helped with the cleanup, just as she always did. After dinner, Hope stepped out onto the front porch and looked at the lawn in the fading light. It definitely needed work, there were plenty of weeds and bare patches. She wasn't sure how to treat it, as the grass was nothing like the grass up north. She was pretty sure the soil wasn't a match either. Her skill set needed to be expanded. As she looked it over, a SUV pulled to the curb and a woman, roughly Hope's age, climbed out and gathered a covered dish from the passenger seat.

Hope waited with a smile. "Hi."

"Hey," the woman said. Black hair framed a round face with big green eyes and the woman carried some extra weight from top to bottom. Hope guessed childbirth had had something to do with that. She came up the steps slowly, as if her legs hurt.

"Are you all right?" Hope asked.

"Oh yes, it's just my stupid hip. I fell a week ago, and it still bothers me. By the way, I'm Jo Ellen Parker. I live down the street. I meant to get here yesterday, but you know how kids are. You mean to fix a casserole, and the next thing you know, you've got one in the emergency room with a broken arm." Jo Ellen smiled.

"Oh my, I hope it's not serious."

"No, he just fell from a tree. Sometimes, I wish Ronnie would hit his head. That might knock some sense into him," the woman kidded.

"Oh, I'm Hope Herring. I have a daughter named Cori, who is tied to her computer at the moment."

"It's like a drug, isn't it?" Jo Ellen shook her head. "I can't seem to tear my kids away from them."

"How many kids do you have?"

"Three, and they're all a trial, just a trial. Here." Jo Ellen held out the dish. "It's not much, but it will keep you fed for a day or two. Is your husband joining you later?"

Hope knew why the woman would ask about a husband. She was still wearing her wedding band, but Hope didn't know how the woman knew her husband wasn't already there.

"My husband died a few months ago," Hope said. "It was one of the reasons we moved."

"Oh my, I'm so sorry. Here I've gone and put my foot in my mouth. That's just like me. I'm forever saying the wrong thing. Please forgive me."

"Nothing to forgive. You couldn't know about Doug. It's perfectly okay."

Hope guessed that Jo Ellen wanted to know the details of Doug's death, and in time, Hope might share those things with her, but not right now, not with someone who kept an eye on the neighborhood and probably shared what she learned.

"Ron, my husband," Jo Ellen said. "He's pretty good around the house so if you need something done on the cheap, give us a call. I wouldn't offer his help, but he's a frustrated engineer. He'd rather get his hands dirty than watch a baseball game, and he loves baseball."

Hope smiled. "Thanks very much. That's good to know. The house is old, so I'm guessing it will have its share of repairs."

The two women stared at each other and Hope knew Jo Ellen wanted to be invited inside so she could look around and get a better idea about the new person in town, but Hope wasn't yet ready for company.

"I have to get going," Jo Ellen said. "Like I said, it's not much, but it's tasty. I hope you like it."

"It's more than enough," Hope said. "And as soon as we get the boxes emptied, you, your husband, and your kids are coming over for a pizza party."

"They would love that. But you better order a mess of pizza. Everyone in my family can eat."

Hope watched Jo Ellen move slowly down the steps and to the car. She guessed that as soon as Jo Ellen reached home, the word would go out about the snooty woman from up north who didn't even have the courtesy to invite people into her home. Hope was pretty sure that the good folk of Castle Park were always invited in. Oh, well. Hope wasn't yet in the hosting mood.

In the kitchen, Hope examined the chicken casserole. It looked more than good enough to eat and it smelled delicious. She slid it into the fridge and joined Cori in the TV room for a few minutes.

"You all right?" Hope asked.

"You keep asking me that," Cori said. "And the answer is still the same. I'm fine."

"Good. I'm going up to my office to straighten up some things. If you need anything, just shout."

"Trust me, I will."

When Hope entered the attic, she was met with a cold draft, which surprised her. Where had the cold air come from? Did she have a leak in her system somewhere? She told herself she didn't need another expense, but she couldn't ignore the problem either. Shaking her head, she walked further into the room. A message on the computer screen stared at her in big red letters...

CME

She blinked, wondering what the message meant and how the message appeared on her screen.

Then, the message disappeared, which seemed even more odd. Messages didn't just appear and disappear at random. Not unless there was something wrong with her computer. That was all she needed, a computer issue. Her heart sank. She was beginning to think that the move wasn't such a good idea after all.

She ran the computer through all the diagnostics she could find. Nothing was wrong according to the programs that tested hardware and software. The computer was as trustworthy as could be. In fact, it seemed to be working faster than before. Did she need to bring in an expert? She thought Cori might know something about computers, but Cori's idea of a solution was a YouTube video, and Hope had to admit that some videos were exactly what was needed.

In the TV room, Hope used her phone to run

through common computer error messages. While there were no lack of error messages, none resembled the two she had seen. She wished she had written down what had been on the screen. In the future, she would make sure to keep a list of the messages that appeared. Sooner or later, she would find one that made sense. Until then, she was going to bed.

7

The bedroom felt the same as it had the previous night. Someone was watching. Hope couldn't shake the feeling, but she was going to try and ignore it. It was her imagination, her feelings of loneliness, the emptiness of missing her husband.

As she stared into the dark, she thought about Jo Ellen who might know a lot about the town and the old house. Hope wanted to know more about the house, especially since Cori had the impression that someone had been in the upstairs hall. While that was disconcerting, it didn't mean she had to sell the house and move away. Since she had a contract with the local school system, she couldn't just pack up and go. No one would ever hire her again if she deserted her position at the school on such short notice. No, she was stuck for the moment.

Heh.

Hope froze. The voice was real ... yet, she knew she was alone in the room. What was going on? She reached out and turned on the bedside lamp. She didn't expect to see anyone, and she didn't. Yet, she had heard something.

Or had she? Hope rubbed at her temple.

New house, new surroundings, couldn't the sounds be misinterpreted? Didn't a cat sometimes sound like a newborn baby? Had she heard a normal house groan and thought it was something else because her mind was wired to hear something human? People sometimes heard what they wanted to hear, not the actual sound. She was certain she had read about such things. People mistook all sorts of sounds for gunfire. Why not a creaking board?

She turned off the lamp and told herself to go to sleep. Her brain was going to make mistakes, especially about sounds. If she started hearing voices, she was destined for the asylum. That thought almost made her laugh. She rolled over and closed her eyes. Sleep would heal her brain ... and her psyche.

The next morning, after breakfast, Hope drove

downtown with Cori. It was only a few blocks, and they could have walked, but Hope didn't want to arrive at the Butter Up Bakery all sweaty and hot. Castle Park in the summer was a hot and humid place.

She parked Cori on a bench not far away, and Hope hurried into the bakery, which smelled as yummy as its name.

"Hello," Hope said to the short, roundish, woman behind the glass counter. "I read online that you're looking for a cake baker. I'd like to apply for the job."

The gray-haired woman eyed Hope up and down. Hope wasn't sure she would pass the inspection.

"What kind of cakes do you bake?"

"Any kind. Bundt, angel food, chocolate, yellow, white, it doesn't matter. I'm fast and I'm good."

"And icing?"

Hope listed a number of icings she could prepare from scratch. "And I decorate also," she said. "I can do virtually any kind of lettering you want. Although, I have to look up words in languages other than English."

"Who doesn't? I don't know you, so if you don't

mind, can you give me some idea of where you live and what you do?"

"Well, I just moved into a house a few blocks from here."

"You're the one? The Johnson house?"

"I don't think so. I bought it from the Wilsons."

"Oh, they lived there recently, but it's still the Johnson house. It will always be the Johnson house."

"Why is that?"

"Because that's the house Maximillian Johnson built over a hundred years ago. It's where he was murdered."

Hope's heart jumped into her throat. "What? You're kidding."

"And the killer was never caught. Not that you have to worry. The killer is long dead by now. How long you been there?"

"Two days," Hope said. "And I have to be honest. I'm a teacher, so when the school year starts, I would have to cut back my hours here at the bakery."

The owner studied Hope for a second. "If the school hired you, then you must be reliable, and that's what I'm looking for. This is the marryin' season and I'm shorthanded, so when do you want to start?"

"Well, I need two more days to sort out the rest of the house. Would that work for you?"

The woman stuck out her hand. "I'm Edsel Morgan. My father gave me a man's name because he thought a girl would be a disappointment. I fooled him."

Hope smiled. "Indeed, you did."

"I'd like you to make a cake as a test," Edsel said. "If it passes, you have the job."

"Okay." Hope smiled. "When should I make the cake for you to sample?"

"Now?"

"Sure. I can do that. I just need to text my daughter. She's waiting for me outside."

"Have her come in," Edsel said. "It's nice and cool in here."

"Thank you. That's very nice." Hope knew she was going to like working there.

After baking the cake, Edsel took a slice and ate it. She closed her eyes and moaned. "Delicious. You're hired."

Hope chatted with the woman for a few more minutes, ironing out pay and duties and what was expected on both sides. Hope found the older woman to be honest and likable, even if a bit rough at times. She smiled thinking that a woman named

Edsel might come with a bit of a chip on her shoulder.

"By the way," Edsel said just as Hope was leaving. "Your first job is going to be a wedding cake. Think you got that in you?"

"No problem," Hope said, although she wasn't terribly sure of her answer. She knew she could bake and ice cakes, and that's all a wedding cake was really ... except there was more of it.

"When do you start?" Cori asked as she and her mother walked along the sidewalk back to the car.

"I start in two days."

"Great. So, what do I do while you're working?"

"I'm thinking the library," Hope said. "Cool, bright, wi-fi, you'll be in heaven."

"Except, I'll be the only one under a hundred years old," Cori said.

Hope laughed. "Anyway, I'm giving you an assignment."

"Homework?" One of Cori's eyebrows went up.

"Yes. Your assignment is to learn all about a man named Maximillian Johnson. He lived in Castle Park some time ago."

"Why do you want to know about him?"

"Because we're living in the house he built."

Cori grinned. "Cool."

"Now, let's find a tech store where I can buy a router booster."

The young clerk in the electronics store was helpful, not overselling like some techies Hope had run into in the past. He was young, knowledgeable, and he didn't overwhelm her with jargon.

The instructions for installing the equipment were simple and straightforward. She and Cori had a good time placing the boosters and downloading the software from the manufacturer's site. Gone were the days when Hope would have loaded some sort of disc. In some ways, life seemed to get easier and easier—provided all the ones and zeroes processed correctly. In a few minutes, Hope had established a connection from her attic office, and that made her smile.

Yet, there was a nagging voice in the back of her mind.

What about the voice I heard?

What about the man Cori saw in the hall?

What about the footsteps I heard in my bedroom?

Hope wanted to ignore everything, but she knew that ignoring certain sounds and feelings wouldn't work. It was like some sort of medical condition. Ignore it, and it simply grew worse, until it couldn't be ignored. Putting off something until it had to be dealt with was not a good strategy.

So, Hope did one more complete search of the house. She paid special attention to doors and windows since they could provide access. She found nothing. The house was as secure as she could make it. Frustrated, she pushed the problem to the back of her mind and went about setting up the rest of the house.

While Hope was no germophobe, she did appreciate a clean house. So, as she set up the rooms, she made sure everything was clean. She didn't want to find anymore dead mice around. And she knew that once she started working at the bakery, she wouldn't have the time for a thorough cleaning. She needed all the work she could get at the bakery.

The cleaning was tiring, which was welcome, because in her down moments, she still wondered about Doug, about what had happened to him, about how it happened, about why it happened. The police explanations were not at all satisfying. She knew there was something they were missing.

At the end of the day, Hope made a spaghetti dinner. She didn't have any meatballs, but the sauce was good enough. It was only after she'd begun the process that she realized that cooking in a Southern summer was not a welcome thing in a house with poor air conditioning. She sweated over the stove and told herself that the air con was one more system due for maintenance. If she was lucky, it would be nothing more than some coolant—if she was lucky.

"Zoe wants to visit," Cori said over dinner.

"Great, but not right away."

"Why not? Summer's almost over."

"Summer's not almost over. And we're not yet ready to host guests."

Cori made a face. "You don't want me to be happy, do you?"

"Happy isn't something I think you should strive for," Hope answered.

"You don't want me to be happy?"

"Happy is a state, and it's only recognizable because people are unhappy a lot of the time. Worse, people often think that happy comes from outside, from the condition of things. If I get a new phone, I'll be happy. If people read my tweets or comments, I'll be happy. If I watch enough TV, I'll be happy."

"That's silly. Watching TV won't make anyone happy."

"You'd be surprised. But I don't think you should

try to *achieve* a state of happiness. What I suggest is that you find things that give you joy."

"Isn't that the same thing?"

"Not really. Joy is what you feel when you find something you love. And it doesn't have to be easy or taste good or depend on someone sending you a happy face. You find things you like to do, love to do. Run, write, read, sing, jog, visit the old, help people. Search for the things that make you smile, that you'll want to do again tomorrow."

Cori stared a moment. "I still think that's the same as happy."

Hope laughed. "Very few ideas are sold on their first attempt."

"Who sells ideas?"

"You know what I mean."

Cori grinned. "Maybe that's where I find joy ... pestering you."

"No doubt, like most kids."

After dinner and clean up, Hope climbed to her attic office for some research on HVAC contractors. It was obvious that North Carolina summers were a bit more intense than Ohio ones. To her pleasant surprise, the router booster worked perfectly. She had no problem accessing or searching the Internet.

In a few minutes, she had assembled a short list

of companies to contact. While she didn't automatically believe the customer reviews, she liked that several companies had both good and not-so-good comments. Any company that received nothing but five stars was suspect, in her opinion. She was about to shut down for the night when she heard a cough.

A cough?

Hope froze. A cough meant a person, and there couldn't be a person in the room with her. That was … impossible. She knew she should turn and look, but she couldn't bring herself to do it. She didn't want to find someone who wasn't her daughter behind her. Her lip quivered. Her fingers trembled. What was going on? She told herself to turn. She ordered herself to turn. She bit her lip and … turned.

The man standing behind her was tall and thin and dressed in clothes from some bygone era. His dark hair was longish, and his beard trimmed. His smile showed slightly yellowed teeth. He seemed unsure of himself, his smile fading and returning, his blue eyes staring.

Hope was absolutely certain she had never seen him before.

"Excuse my manners," the man said right before he disappeared.

That was when everything went black.

8

"Mom? Mom?"

Hope heard the voice, a voice she recognized, yet, she couldn't see her daughter. Why was that?

"Open your eyes," Cori said.

Hope opened her eyes to see her daughter hovering over her.

"Are you all right?" Cori asked, her face full of worry.

"I ... I think so," Hope answered, rubbing the side of her face. She looked past Cori. The attic office looked exactly as she thought it should. If she remembered, she should be in the office, but not on the floor, which was where she was.

"I called, and when you didn't answer, I came up. What are you doing on the floor?"

Hope blinked and wondered for a moment. Then, she remembered the man in the old-fashioned clothes, the bearded man with blue eyes. The man who had spoken to her.

"Did you see someone?" Hope asked.

"See someone?"

"Help me up."

With Cori's help, Hope managed to stand and sit back down in her desk chair. While she expected the room to spin, it didn't. It was as stable as always.

"What's wrong?" Cori asked.

"Nothing. Nothing's wrong. I … just … fainted."

"Fainted? No one faints anymore. What would make you faint?" Cori stared at her mother.

"I guess I tried to get up too fast. You know, well, maybe you don't know, but if you've been sitting for a long time, and you get up too fast, sometimes you get dizzy."

"I never do."

"Well, no, you're too young. Sometimes, it happens to older people."

"You're not old."

"Not too old. Let me rest for a second or two."

"What can I get you? Want some water?"

"In a minute."

Hope worked to organize her thoughts. She

remembered what had happened, sort of. But now that Cori was there, she thought the sequence could have been reversed. Maybe she fainted, and *then*, she saw the bearded man. That made sense. The man was just some sort of dream or illusion.

But why had she fainted in the first place?

It was a question she couldn't answer. She didn't remember trying to get up or feeling dizzy. She remembered a … cough.

Hope's heart began to race, but she tried to shake off her fear. The cough she heard had to have been part of the dream, too. She'd fainted and imagined the rest of it.

She held out her hand, and Cori pulled.

"Thanks," Hope said. "I'm fine now. Let's have some ice cream. Maybe my blood sugar got low."

Cori stared. "Are you sure? Are you going to fall down the stairs, because if you are, then you can't walk down. You have to sit on the stairs and scoot down on your butt. I know, I saw it on some YouTube video."

"I'm not going to fall down the steps," Hope said. "I really do feel normal, but if it will make you feel better, I'll let you go first. That way, I'll fall on you."

"Oh, great, then we can both break our necks."

"Life is filled with uncertainty," Hope kidded.

"Right."

Hope followed Cori down to the first floor where they both sat at the kitchen table and ate ice cream.

"I think I'm just tired from the move and trying to get the house set up," Hope said.

Cori looked up at her mother. "I know, Mom. Things haven't been easy. We're doing okay."

Her daughter's words filled Hope's heart with warmth. She smiled weakly and gave Cori a nod.

After that, it was time for bed. Cori followed Hope up the steps in case her mother felt dizzy again, but Hope wasn't about to faint, she felt fine. She wondered again how she'd fainted earlier. She could only remember passing out once before when she was around twelve when she cut herself and saw the blood.

It was just all the stress she'd been dealing with and the sudden movement of standing up. It could happen to anyone, especially someone who was in the throes of losing her husband, moving to a new town, buying a new house, and starting a new job.

"I know what you're thinking," Hope said. "You're thinking I have some medical condition. You think I have a brain tumor or something, but I don't."

"Almost no one with a brain tumor thinks they have a brain tumor," Cori said. "I read that."

"In my case, it's true, but I promise, if I faint again, I'll go to the doctor, okay?"

Cori thought for a second. "Fair enough, but I'm going to ask you questions every day."

"What kind of questions?"

"Memory questions. I read that people with brain tumors often forget simple things, like what they had for breakfast, their old phone numbers and addresses. Brain issues can weaken memory."

"Sure," Hope said. "But it works both ways. If you forget things that I ask you about then I'll take *you* to the doctor."

"I'm not the one who fainted."

"But you might be the one who forgets."

"All right," Cori said. "I'm still going to worry about you."

"I'm okay. Now, go to bed." Hope smiled and kissed her daughter on the head.

As she watched Cori disappear into her room, Hope realized she herself shared a bit of her daughter's fear. Since fainting was not part of her normal life, she thought maybe there was something going on with her physical health. After all, she'd heard things in the house, things that if she admitted to, Cori would force Hope to the emergency room. So, she decided she was going to keep those things to herself ... for now.

Pulling the blanket around her, Hope sat up in bed for a moment and wondered if she should leave the light on. That would make her feel a bit better, but it would also be giving in to her fear.

But which fear?

Was it the fear of someone in the house, something that she'd proven couldn't be true? Or, was it the fear that there was something physically wrong with her?

With a groan, she shook her head. She was being silly. She'd slept in the dark since she was seven years old. She wasn't going to believe in the bogeyman now. She turned off the light and lay still, listening. She couldn't help it, she had to listen. She hoped she wouldn't dream about the bearded man with the blue eyes.

In the middle of the night, Hope woke with a start from a feeling that someone had been standing over her, staring. Her eyes could make out shapes in the dim light, so she knew that couldn't be true. There wasn't anyone in the room. Yet, she felt it ... she felt it deep inside. It was a crazy thought. She sighed with frustration at her silly thoughts and soon, she was asleep again.

9

Hope was convinced that if Cori really believed her mother had a brain tumor, she would have been waiting at the stairs the next morning to be sure Hope didn't fall down the staircase. Thankfully, Cori was still in bed.

Hope had to navigate the descent without her daughter on the next step down. It made her chuckle. She was on her second cup of coffee by the time Cori woke up and came into the kitchen.

"I was going to lead you down the stairs," Cori said with a yawn. "You should have waited for me."

"You're too late. I was able to manage on my own," Hope kidded. "Now, do you believe I'm all right?"

"I'm not convinced, yet," Cori said. "What's for breakfast?"

"Whatever you can find to eat," Hope answered. "And you have exactly ten minutes to add whatever you want to the grocery list."

"Whatever I want?"

"Within reason. You know there are some things I won't buy."

"That's dictatorship."

Hope grinned. "It's about time you recognized that."

While Cori thought about what she might want from the store, Hope went to her bedroom for her purse and saw that the top wasn't zippered. She blinked. She always left it closed. It was a habit she'd started a few years ago after someone lifted her wallet from her open purse.

She stared at her open purse. She must have forgotten to close it. She told herself she needed to get more sleep.

In the grocery store aisle, Hope ran into Jo Ellen.

"How is the moving-in going?" Jo Ellen asked.

"Slow, but we're getting there." Hope glanced round. "Are your kids with you?"

"They're at home. The oldest looks after the

others, and with any luck, one of them will be dead and buried by the time I get back."

Hope laughed along with Jo Ellen.

"I'm only half joking," Jo Ellen continued. "They're a handful, and if it wasn't for this *me* time, I'd go insane. You have no idea what they can get into."

"Kids are kids, I guess."

"And mine love soda, which is why I give them milk." Jo Ellen chuckled. "They don't like it as much, but it's better for them. I just wish it was cheaper."

"Don't give them too much. They'll grow up too fast."

"If that moves them out of the house sooner, I'll force feed them."

Hope went up and down the grocery store's aisles with Jo Ellen, listening to the antics of her children and her husband. It seemed that her husband got into as much trouble as the kids. She suspected that Jo Ellen needed to vent, and Hope was content to listen.

"How's the house?" Jo Ellen asked as they crossed the parking lot together.

"So far, so good," Hope answered.

"Nothing strange?"

One of Hope's eyebrows raised. "Strange how?"

J. A. WHITING & NELL MCCARTHY

"Well," Jo Ellen hedged. "The last family that lived there had some rather colorful stories."

"Such as?"

"Nothing I would repeat. I don't want to put ideas into anyone's head."

"You can't very well stop now," Hope said. "What kind of stories did you hear?"

"Well, for one, it seemed Crystal, that was the mom, was always having her purse looked into."

"Looked into?" A shiver of unease ran down Hope's back.

"You know, things moved from one pocket to another. Nothing was ever missing. It was just someone wanting to play games. Her children and husband always denied it, but one of them had to be the culprit."

"It must have been one of them," Hope said, but wasn't so sure.

"Crystal hid her purse one night in a place she didn't think her children knew anything about, but the purse was still handled by someone."

Hope swallowed. "It's hard to fool kids."

"The only time it wasn't messed with was when she locked it in her car. You would think the kids would know how to get around a simple lock, but they didn't."

"Or, maybe they just wanted to keep their mother guessing."

"I suggested fingerprints, but I suppose that wouldn't do much good. The others' fingerprints would naturally be on the purse."

With a wave and a goodbye, Jo Ellen went to her car, but Hope kept thinking about the purse story. Her own purse was open when she went to get it that morning. Had Cori gone through it? Was that what woke her the night before? Hope shook her head. She was letting her mind run away with silly ideas after listening to Jo Ellen's story.

Hope spent the rest of the day in her attic office where she went over her paperwork. She needed to file away the house papers, the bank account papers, the credit card papers, and the files for all the utilities. Owning a home wasn't just a matter of making mortgage payments. There were a million small things that needed attention. If she wasn't organized, something would fall through the cracks, and she would have a real problem on her hands.

As the sun settled behind the trees, her back hurt, and her stomach growled. It was time for dinner. After that, she would arrange for the next day, the library for Cori and the Butter Up Bakery for her. Her first day at the new job filled her with a little bit of fear.

"Tomorrow," Hope said to her daughter, "we're good to go, right? Library for you, work for me."

"What should I do for lunch?" Cori asked.

"There's a diner and a burger place just a block from the library. You can take your pick, but don't go anywhere else. And you know all the other rules."

Cori rolled her eyes. "Don't talk to strangers, don't eat too much junk, and don't get into any vans unless they really look cool."

"Ha ha," Hope deadpanned.

"I mean it. In all the movies, the bad guys always have dingy, dirty vans. A clean van is fine to get into," Cori teased her mother.

"You're not funny."

"Okay, no vans. How about a Corvette? Or what about a Porsche? Can I get into a Porsche?"

Hope shook her head. "You know what? I'm tempted to say go ahead. Having one less mouth to feed would help me out."

"Now, *you're* not funny," Cori said.

"I'm always funny. And don't forget it."

The evening passed quickly. Cori forgot all about escorting Hope up and down the stairs. That had been a one-time event, which was fine with Hope.

The last thing she wanted was a shadow ... or for her daughter to worry about her.

In her bedroom, Hope laid her purse on a chair and hesitated. She wasn't ready to lock it inside her car. Did she just forget to close the top of the purse last night? Did Cori go into it for some reason? Cori never did that. Hope shook her head, then took the purse, made sure to close it, and put it in one of her bureau drawers.

She rested her head on her pillow and fell asleep without feeling she was under someone's gaze. She recognized that her previous feeling was simply the concern of being in some place new, from being forced to start over without her husband. She supposed that after a week or two, she wouldn't notice the house's noises.

The next morning, Hope dressed for work, which meant jeans and a T-shirt. She wouldn't be working the bakery counter and if she was going to get flour all over her clothes, she wasn't going to wear anything nice. She was just the cake maker.

Hope spent a few seconds wondering about her purse before she remembered that she had put it in the bureau for safekeeping. She chuckled as she pulled it out, still zipped up tight. The previous day had been nothing but a small hiccup. She almost felt a sort of joy.

Hope watched Cori head into the library after she'd promised to text before she left for lunch. Hope still trusted libraries, especially small-town libraries. People might be nosier in small towns, but they were also more observant. Cori would be safe there.

Edsel smiled when Hope entered the bakery. "I wasn't sure you'd show up," the woman said.

"I need the money," Hope answered with a smile.

"Don't we all." Edsel shook her head.

With some friendly small talk and after Edsel had shown her around the kitchen, Hope went to work.

The wedding cake was a special order. The bottom layer would be yellow cake, the middle tier would be chocolate, and the top tier would be red velvet. Hope didn't know who had chosen the colors or flavors, and it didn't matter. Edsel pointed out where the ingredients were and the equipment was, and that was all Hope needed.

Hope had always been an excellent baker, and she supposed that had she not gone into teaching, she might have opened a bakery of her own. There wasn't much about baking that she didn't know or couldn't learn. Cakes were a specialty, but she could make donuts and pies and muffins and breads and filled-pastries of all sorts. It was fun, but most of the time, she was thankful that she hadn't gone into the baking business because she guessed she would have gained about a hundred pounds if she owned her own bakery. Good bakers needed to sample their creations.

The cakes went into the oven before lunch. True to her word, Cori texted that she was going for a burger and would text again when she returned to the library. Hope told herself that things were working out just as she hoped. She was sipping a cup of coffee when Edsel walked in from the front.

"Come with me," Edsel said with a wink. "Someone wants to meet you."

10

"Who would want to meet me?" Hope asked.

"The mother of the bride."

Sandra Remby was Hope's idea of a mother trying too hard. Thin, blond hair, bleached eyebrows, hazel eyes, and bright red lips, Sandra reminded Hope of someone searching for youth. Sandra's skin was dark from a chemical tan, not the sun, and the loose skin under her chin testified to perhaps a quick, hard diet. But even so, Sandra was an attractive woman. Her perfectly tailored outfit implied that Sandra had money, and her white teeth gleamed as she smiled.

"I'm Sandra Remby," the woman said. "Mother of Carter, the bride. I just wanted to stop in and chat for a moment."

"I'm glad you did," Hope said cheerfully. "I've just started on the cake."

"That's so good to hear. I can't believe the wedding will be here in two days. Edsel did acquaint you with the colors and the decorations we picked out for the cake, didn't she?"

"She did, and I promise you the cake will meet your specifications ... and, it will taste delicious."

"That is so good to hear. You would not believe how difficult the last cake maker was. I couldn't get her to understand the need for perfection. You do understand the need for perfection, don't you?"

"I certainly do," Hope said. "And if you'd like to come in Friday night for an inspection, I'll be happy to show it to you."

"Oh, hon, I would, but that's the rehearsal dinner night. I can't possibly be here."

"Well, I could text a picture of the cake to you. I'd be happy to send you one."

Hope looked past Sandra to Edsel, whose cheeks were bright red.

"Would you do that for me?" Sandra asked. "Why that's the best thing ever." She turned to Edsel. "Isn't that the best thing ever?"

"It is," Edsel muttered.

"You're new to town, aren't you?" Sandra asked.

"I am," Hope admitted. "I bought the old Johnson house."

Sandra's eyes opened wider. "Did you? Didn't anyone tell you about that old place?"

A flurry of nervousness flitted over Hope's skin. "Tell me what?"

"Why, it's haunted, of course. Everyone in town knows it's haunted."

"It's not haunted," Edsel said. "It's just a bunch of people *wanting* it to be haunted."

Sandra leveled her eyes at Edsel. "Why, that's nice of you to say, but we both know that house has been spooked for many, many decades."

Hope wasn't sure how to take things, so, she just smiled politely.

"But I'm happy someone is living in that drafty, old place. It would be a shame if it fell into ruin. I'm sure the ghost won't bother you," Sandra said.

"I'm sure it won't," Hope said. "By the way, does this ghost have a name?"

"Oh, I don't know anything about that," Sandra said. "You'll send me a picture of the cake on Friday?"

"I'll be sure to do it," Hope said.

After Sandra left, Edsel turned to Hope. "You can send that picture, but I don't think it's a good idea.

She is way too picky and controlling. You know she's going find something wrong with it and then you'll have to fix it before the wedding."

Hope smiled. "I know she will, and when I fix what she wants fixed, she'll brag about the Butter Up Bakery to all her friends. Especially, those with daughters."

"I hope you're right, but I really think you're going to be chasing your tail until it's time to haul the cake to the reception. I need you to deliver the cake so you can put any last finishing touches on it."

With a smile, Hope asked, "Or do you mean I'll be doing the delivering so I'll be the one who takes the heat when Sandra has some complaining to do?"

"Maybe."

Hope laughed. "Of course, I'll bring the cake if you want me to, but I don't have to stay the whole time, do I?"

"No, once they cut the cake, you're free to go. I just don't want some child running a finger through the icing or knocking it over or whatever. Protect it until the bride and groom cut it, then leave."

"Okay, sounds good."

All afternoon, Hope tried to work out how she was going to get care for Cori during the reception. She didn't like leaving her alone at the house since they didn't really know anyone in town yet. There was the library, but Hope didn't know what Saturday hours would cover. Then, she decided she would simply put Cori in a dress and bring her along. No one would notice or care. Hope was pretty sure Cori would enjoy it. Some kids liked weddings and receptions.

After the cakes came out of the oven, Hope carefully wrapped them and put them in the cooler. She would ice them later. As long as the cake was finished by Friday evening, she would be able to please Sandra and Edsel. She started to wonder just what a cake baker wore to a reception, but she chased the thought from her mind. She didn't need to worry about it. She supposed any dress would do since she wouldn't be there very long.

"Nice work," Edsel said as Hope prepared to leave. "Finish tomorrow?"

"You bet. It will be ready for a picture and Sandra's inspection."

Edsel chuckled. "You're not going to give her much time to study it, are you?"

"I'm guessing she'll be very busy at the rehearsal dinner. She won't have much time for criticism. I hope."

"That works for me. See you tomorrow. Good work today, Hope."

As Hope walked to the library, she thought about Sandra's insistence that Hope's house was haunted. What made her think that? Sure, the man who built the house was murdered there. But that was almost a century earlier. Ghosts didn't hang around that long, did they? Maybe, Sandra was simply trying to get inside Hope's head, trying to plant some seed. It wasn't as if the former owners were fearful of the house. It wasn't as if they had gone running out of the place, shouting "Ghost! Ghost!" Hope wasn't going to buy into Sandra's talk.

She found Cori in a corner, reading a book, a real book. That surprised her ... she expected Cori to be bent over her phone or maybe staring into a computer screen.

"Couldn't find the electronic copy?" Hope asked with a smile.

"Sometimes, your eyes feel better when you look at paper instead of a screen."

"Someone told you that once upon a time," Hope grinned.

"Who listens?"

"Exactly."

On the way home, Hope decided they'd have

soup and bread for dinner since Cori had already had a burger. Soup was simple and easy. Hope didn't feel like taking on anything difficult, not after baking for most of the day.

She started the soup simmering before she went for a shower. The hot water felt good on her skin and relaxed her muscles. After toweling off, she breezed into her bedroom and suddenly stopped.

Her purse.

In the chair.

It was wide open.

Hope stared. She was certain she'd left the purse closed and clasped.

Who had opened it?

The only person who could have opened the purse was Cori. That was the simple part. The difficult part was *why*. Why had Cori messed with the purse? Had she taken something? If not, why get into the purse at all?

Did she need money?

While Cori didn't have the biggest allowance, she certainly had enough. And she had never taken money in the past without asking.

What other reason could there be?

None.

Hope had no choice. She pulled out her wallet

and counted her money. She was missing absolutely nothing. As far as she knew, she had every penny she should have. But if Cori wasn't after money, what else was there? Hope frowned, because the only way to know was to ask.

"Hey," Hope said when she was back in the kitchen.

Cori looked up from the kitchen table, where she was busy with her tablet.

"Any particular reason you were in my purse?"

Cori looked dumbfounded. "In your purse? I wasn't in your purse."

Hope said, "Did you need something? My purse has been unzipped twice in the past couple of days. Were you looking for something?"

"I don't lie," Cori said. "I wasn't in your purse."

Cori's insistence stymied Hope who could almost always flag a lie when she heard one. She never would have made it as a teacher, if she couldn't tell when a student claimed, "the dog ate my homework." She was inclined to believe her daughter, but that defied the logic involved. The purse had been opened while she was in the shower, and since they were the only two people in the house ... Hope was pretty sure she hadn't opened the purse and forgotten about it.

Hope asked, "Have you seen anyone in the house?"

Cori's eyes widened. "There's someone in the house?"

"I don't think so. Have you seen someone walking around outside in the yard?"

Cori shook her head. "What is this about?"

"When I put down my purse, it was closed. When I came out of the shower, it was open. I didn't open it. If you didn't, then, maybe someone came into the house."

Cori looked over her shoulder. "It wasn't me. Are you sure it was closed? Maybe you think you closed it, but you didn't."

Hope tried to remember how she'd entered the bedroom. She was sure the purse was closed. "All right," Hope said. "For the moment, let's just say I'm mistaken, and I could be. But I want you to be on the lookout for anything out of the ordinary."

"Like what?" Cori's voice seemed to shake a little.

"Like finding something out of place, like a jacket not where you thought you left it. Or, your phone isn't where you put it. Or maybe the last number you called changed. You know, where the present doesn't match your memory."

"You're scaring me."

"I'm just asking you to be mindful of things, of details. I can't explain anything at the moment. I don't know why I'm finding things different from how I left them. I just am, and it's unsettling. So, I want you to be on the lookout. I want you to tell me if it happens to you."

"I will. But is there someone in the house with us?"

"No. I've checked."

"Do you think someone broke in when we were out?"

Hope sighed. "I just don't know. I don't think so."

"Do you think I should lock my bedroom door at night?"

"It wouldn't hurt."

Hope held out her arms and Cori came for a hug. "I'm probably just being silly," she told her daughter.

"I sure hope so."

Hope kept the conversation light during dinner. There was no more talk about paying attention to details or other people in the house. They talked about the book Cori was reading, how the book felt good in her hands. There was just something about a book that a tablet or a laptop couldn't duplicate.

After dinner, Hope made sure all the doors were double locked before she went to her attic office. She hadn't been there since her blackout moment when she'd dreamt of the bearded man.

She made sure all the lights were on before she sat at her computer and she even made sure the door behind her was closed. She didn't want anyone to sneak up on her. Hope couldn't help but glance over her shoulder every minute or two which was pretty silly, she decided. She told herself she was getting paranoid. Paranoia was all she needed on top of everything else. What had she done? This was not why she left Ohio. She tried to focus, and spent an hour on some paperwork and paying some bills.

"Back to the library tomorrow," Hope said, as she tucked in Cori. "Enjoying the book?"

"Yeah, I'm almost finished," Cori answered.

"Will you go to the diner for lunch?"

"I don't know. The burger was pretty good."

"Get some sleep, hon."

"You too, Mom."

"Love you. See you in the morning."

Back in her room, Hope was mindful enough to put her purse in the bureau drawer. She was tempted to use her phone to take a photo of the purse, but she thought that was going too far. What was next? Taking photos of her bedroom? Her car? She chided herself for being so foolish. Her brain must be playing tricks on her, because Cori wasn't suffering the same events. It had to be all the stress she'd been under.

But Cori's fear might be true. Maybe Hope was suffering from some sort of physical affliction, maybe something that affected her short-term memory. Could that be the reason for the unusual things that had been happening?

She shook herself. Nothing was wrong with her. Her brain was fine. She was just worried about so many things. It was stress and not paying attention to what she was doing.

Hope locked her bedroom door before she shut off the light. Lying in bed, she closed her eyes and tried to feel calm. She didn't hear anything strange and she didn't sense anyone else in the room. Breathing a sigh of relief, she rolled over and went to sleep.

In the morning, the first thing Hope did was go to the bureau where she pulled out the drawer and checked her purse.

Then, she began to shake.

11

The purse was totally and perfectly clasped. It was what was on top of the purse that made Hope shake. It was a ... mouse. A dead mouse.

It had to be dead because it wasn't moving, and a live mouse would have tried to escape.

A dead mouse.

How had the mouse invaded the drawer?

Hope supposed there were a number of ways a mouse could have gotten inside the drawer. Mice were supple and clever. They could get through spaces far too small for other creatures. But why her drawer? It wasn't as if there was food to be found. And on top of her purse? That seemed highly improbable, and yet, there was the small, gray mouse with its black, dead eyes.

Hope stopped shaking and did what had to be done with the mouse. She was glad she could dispose of it before Cori woke up. Another mouse and no cat might have set off Cori. Hope was pretty sure everyone would be better off if the mouse could simply be forgotten.

The second cup of coffee transformed Hope's internal shakes into external ones, which was fine with her. She knew she would have to stop at two cups since she had more than a bit of decorating to perform at the bakery and a quivering hand was not a welcome issue. That made her wonder how many doctors drank coffee before surgery? Did operating room mistakes owe their origins to caffeine? That was another reason to avoid the hospital.

Cori seemed to be in a fog as she ate breakfast. She didn't fully wake until she was dropped off at the library, with the usual admonishments and promises from her mother. Hope was certain Cori could be trusted to avoid trouble.

When she arrived at the bakery, the flow of customers had already started and Edsel was preoccupied and busy. She and Hope exchanged "hellos" but that was the extent of their conversation. Hope headed to the back workroom, slipped an apron over her head, and took out some ingredients and a big bowl.

For Hope, the secret to icing a cake was the sugar. It was the taste that made all the difference. People would forgive a less-than-inspired decoration if the icing tasted great, and great taste came from sugar. It was that simple. She thanked her mother for the taste buds she used to determine the proper amount of sweetener. Precise measurement was needed, but the proof of the icing was in the taste.

Once the icing was smooth and pleasing, Hope went to work on the coloring.

Colors were one reason why Hope had no love for wedding planners. It seemed that wedding planners steered brides toward exotic colors that were difficult to pronounce and impossible to match perfectly. She guessed that the bride sat down with a stack of paint swatches and tried to decide between periwinkle blue and cerulean. There wouldn't be three attendees at the wedding who could tell the difference, and yet, Hope was pretty sure that Carter's planner would bring out a swatch to compare to the icing.

Hope knew that some cake makers used charts to combine basic dyes into the desired color. She understood the mixing, but she relied more on her vision than the chart. Besides, not every possible color came with a ready-made ingredients chart. Yet, she managed to achieve the shades she wanted. While the basic icing would be white, the roses and other details would be in the prescribed colors.

Hope removed the bottom layer of the wedding cake, made certain it was undamaged, and set it on its base for decorating. The icing was ready, and she went to work. This was the moment of truth for her. She had to work at a good pace, and she had to be exact. Edsel would end Hope's employment if Sandra found the cake wanting.

Hope spent the morning on the cake, and by lunchtime, she was ready to put it away for a bit. She was something of a perfectionist, but she knew she could not spend hours on end with the cake. If she did that, it would only suffer in the end. She wheeled it into the cooler. Then, Hope went outside for lunch into the heat and humidity of a North Carolina, low country summer.

Her phone showed her that Cori had returned to the burger place, and while Hope loved her daughter, she needed a bit of down time. Trading chat with Cori didn't seem like the way to forget the wedding cake for thirty minutes so she headed to the nearby diner to have a quiet lunch.

The place was full, but Hope found a stool at the counter. Obviously, the Sunrise Cafe was popular with the downtown crowd. The man next to her, an older gentleman wearing a starched shirt and tie, moved his newspaper to make room for her. She nodded a thanks and picked up a menu.

"Excuse me," the man said. "You just moved into the old Johnson place, right?"

"That's me," Hope replied. "Hope Herring."

"Harley Story." The man stuck out his hand. "My middle name is Quinn. My parents had a wicked sense of humor."

With a smile, Hope shook the man's hand. "Pleased to meet you."

"I'm an accountant," Harley continued. "My office is around the corner if you ever need my services." He pulled a small, leather holder from his pocket and took out a card. "I do taxes for individuals and small businesses, and I like to think I save my clients a fair amount of money. No one likes to pay the government more than what is absolutely due."

"I agree with that." Hope placed the card in her

J. A. WHITING & NELL MCCARTHY

purse. The man was older, pushing sixty. His mostly gray hair was thin and combed over, but not in any offensive way. His dark brown eyes looked a little distorted in his trifocal glasses. His smile was pleasant and encouraging and laugh lines surrounded his mouth. He seemed genuine and interested.

"I'm a local. Been here all my life, except for some time in the Army. Castle Park is a nice, little community. I think you'll find people friendly, for the most part. But you know how things are in a small town. Rumor is the usual stock in trade." He chuckled.

Hope laughed. "I'm aware, and I appreciate the advice. Since I have a move to contend with this tax year, I might well contact you about handling my taxes."

"Pleased to help. The Johnson house should be worth some deductions, I would think."

"It seems everyone knows the place," she said. "What can you tell me about it?"

"Well, I can tell you that when I was a boy, we used to sneak out of the house at midnight and run down to the house to look for the blue lights."

"Blue lights?"

"There was a belief that the house was haunted, and that at midnight on some nights, strange blue lights would appear in the attic window. It was supposed to be the ghost. Well, I can tell you that I spent more than one midnight staring at that window, and I never spotted any blue lights."

"Well, it was a fun adventure." Hope sipped from a mug of coffee.

"Oh yes, it was an opportunity to disobey without really taking any risk. I always thought I had fooled my parents, but I'm pretty sure they knew what I was up to."

"Parents generally do. Did anyone ever see the blue lights?"

"Not that I know of. Of course, that was when the house was vacant. After people started living in it, no one ever mentioned the lights anymore."

"So, is there anything else I need to know about the house?" Hope asked.

"Not really. Over the years, there have been times when the ghost story surfaces. You understand how such stories cycle. Seems as if every generation needs to resurrect it."

"But the original owner was murdered there, right?"

"Indeed, he was. It's our own favorite mystery. No one was ever arrested or tried. If you want to know more about it, Margaret Kinston is our local historian. She knows as much as anyone. She lives over on Maple, but you're just as likely to find her at the old railroad depot."

"A train goes through here?"

"Not anymore. Trains disappeared from Castle Park some time ago, along with the boats that used to come up river. The historical society office is in the old depot. This town has a bit of history, including a revolutionary war battle that happened not too far away. But I'm getting ahead of myself. Talk to Margaret sometime, if you want a thorough recap of the murder. And now, I better get back to work. By the way, you smell like donuts." Harley smiled.

Hope laughed. "I'm working at the Butter Up Bakery until school starts. I'll be teaching then, but I'll probably still work weekends at the bakery. Being a single parent requires money."

"Don't I know it. And if you wish to maximize the return on your taxes, give me a shout. I think you'll find my rates reasonable."

Hope watched Harley walk out, and she wondered if he was married. He wore a ring, so the answer was probably yes. And she guessed that, in time, she would meet his wife. In small towns, people met everyone else at one time or another.

She tried to picture a young Harley running down a dark sidewalk with his friends, heading for the house of "blue lights," the haunted house that had never been haunted.

She hoped.

12
___

"What will it be?"

Hope smiled out of her reverie and turned to the waitress. "How about a BLT?" she asked.

"Want anything else to drink, hon?" The waitress smiled and waited, as if she had all the time in the world. That was another thing about the South. People took their time.

"Lemonade, please," Hope answered.

The afternoon was dedicated to the cake. Hope mixed and tasted and applied, and in the end, the three-tier cake looked magnificent.

"That's as good as it gets," Edsel said when she saw it. "You have the knack."

Hope took several photos of the cake. "I hope Sandra agrees."

"She better. That's a sight better than she could get anywhere else."

"I'll send you her comments," Hope said, smiling.

"Not that I want to read them. But send them to me anyway. I always need something to fire me up."

Cori was waiting on the bench outside the library when Hope arrived.

"Finish your book?" Hope asked.

"Yeah. I got cold in the library so I came outside," Cori replied. "The sun felt good ... for about a minute. Now I'm too hot."

Hope laughed. "I guess that's the way it is down here. You stay inside and get nice and cool, and then, the sun feels great, but not for long. Learn anything today?"

"I learned that this is hurricane season. We're right in the middle of it."

"But we're not on the coast."

"No, but we're close. Will said Castle Park has been hit by a lot of hurricanes."

"Who's Will?" Hope asked.

"Oh, his real name is Wilton, and he lives on Walnut Street. He likes to read. He's not real big and doesn't do sports. He's more of a nerd."

"He's your age?"

"Yeah, we might be in the same class. He says school is all right, but sometimes, it's boring."

"Anything can be boring at times. The trick is to find ways not to be bored."

"Easy for you to say."

In Ohio, Hope and Cori often enjoyed a night out together. It was a way to wind down after the work week. Hope wanted to continue the tradition here in the new town. Moving to a new state didn't mean getting rid of all the little things they had done before, but she wasn't sure where to go. She supposed the best bet was the Applebee's by the Interstate. While it might lack local flavor, it was familiar.

"Applebee's is fine," Cori said. "I like their salads."

"Done, and done," Hope said.

Hope allowed herself one drink with her dinner. She liked white wine, and she found a vintage that appealed to her. But she had only one glass. She was well aware of the drunk driving laws. The last thing she needed was a citation.

At the house, she drank a second glass, as she didn't have to get up early. The cake had to be delivered to the country club at the proper hour, and she had to hang around until it was cut and tasted.

"By the way," Hope said, as she settled down with Cori to watch TV. "You have to come with me tomorrow to a wedding reception."

"Me?"

"Yep. I made the cake, and the mother of the bride wants me there in case the cake doesn't please. It's a pain, but I said I'd do it. So, you get to put on a dress and come with me."

"But, I don't know anyone."

"I don't either. We won't be there long."

"I don't really want to go."

Hope shook her head. "I know, but I don't want to leave you here alone, and the library closes early tomorrow so you have to come along."

"Can I sit in the car?"

"I'm not sure how long I'll be. Look at it as an opportunity. You get the chance to see a wedding reception."

"I've seen one already."

"I know, but that was up north. This will be a Southern wedding reception."

"There's a difference?"

"People have all sorts of local traditions. Maybe it will be interesting."

Cori frowned, but Hope could tell that her daughter was warming to the idea. That was a good thing. Hope didn't need an angry daughter at the reception.

"And I'm sure there will be other kids your age there," Hope added. She didn't want to point out that they probably wouldn't be there long enough for Cori to actually meet anyone.

The TV show didn't really interest Hope, so she took her wine and headed for her office. She needed to send the cake photos to Sandra and then wait for the reply. With any luck, Sandra would be too busy to do anything but glance at the pictures. Hope liked that idea.

She settled behind her desk and crossed her fingers as she sent the photos in a text. Then, she put the phone down and brought her computer to life. Email had become something of a chore for her. Almost everything in her inbox file was junk, but it still had to be handled. It took time to go through all of it. She was halfway through the list when she heard the voice.

"Don't faint," someone said.

Hope dropped her wine glass and spun around towards the voice.

The bearded man looked back at her, the same

man she had seen in what she thought was a dream. Hope stared, even as her wine-shaded brain tried to take in what was going on. She blinked several times, as if the man would disappear, as if he was just some sort of a floater in her vision.

"You might want to retrieve your glass," the man said and pointed to the carpet.

Flustered, Hope snatched up her glass, mindful that the wine was seeping into the carpet.

"And you need a towel," the man added.

"W... who are you?" Hope asked, ignoring the wine. "What are you doing in my house?"

"I would think that was obvious," the man said. "My name is, was, no, is I suppose, Maximillian Johnson, and this is still my house, seeing as I'm the one who had it built. I've lived here quite a bit longer than you have."

With her heart pounding, Hope closed her eyes. "He's not here," she whispered. "He's just a figment of my imagination. He's something my mind made up."

"I'm not a figment," the man said.

"It's the wine and the pressure and the move and losing Doug and everything. My brain is scrambled."

"Your brain is perfectly all right. I'm just a ghost, pure and simple."

"No, no, no," Hope said, her eyes still closed. "There are no such things as ghosts."

"There certainly are, because here I am."

"It's just stress and worry." Hope clasped her hands together tightly.

"You're not listening."

"Perhaps, the mushrooms were tainted." Hope stopped and listened for a second. She heard nothing, and that was a good sign, a very good sign. She opened her eyes. The bearded man was gone. She smiled.

"Are you quite past your denial?" a voice asked.

She wheeled around to see the bearded man standing by the window.

"This can't be happening. Am I losing my mind?" Hope's eyes watered and she started to tremble.

"I told myself that this was a bad idea," the ghost muttered. "I mean how could I expect someone to believe me? No one believes in ghosts any more, no matter what we do. You would think the purse would have been enough, at least a hint."

"Please go away," Hope said. "I don't care who or what you are. I need you to go away." She paused and tapped her forehead. "I'm talking as if he's really here. How crazy am I?"

"You're not disturbed at all. You simply need to

toss aside your disbelief for a moment and embrace what is happening. I am here, and I am a ghost."

Hope looked at the wine glass. "Did someone put something in my wine? Are there drugs in my wine? Is that what's causing this ... vision?"

"I would remind you that there is only you and your daughter in the house. Well, there's me also, but I hardly count. So, unless you're prepared to accuse your daughter, you can rest assured that your wine was not doctored in any way."

With beads of perspiration showing on her forehead, Hope stood and looked about. "I need to get out of here."

"I wish you wouldn't go. Trust me, this is no easier for me than it is for you, but I am making the effort. I need to talk to you."

Hope started for the door. "Maybe it's some kind of poisonous gas in the air, some undetectable gas. Like radon. That's it, there must be radon in the air."

"I have no idea what radon is, but there is no gas or potion troubling you. It's simply me. I wish to establish contact with you."

"And voices. I've never heard voices before. Cori was right. There must be something wrong with me." A few tears ran down Hope's cheeks.

"I just want to talk to you. I mean no harm. I would think the mice would indicate that."

Hope stopped and turned to the bearded man. "You left the dead mice?!"

13

"Don't look at me that way," the bearded man said. "They weren't alive. I would think you would thank me for keeping the house free of dead mice. You would not believe how persistent the little creatures can be, especially in the winter. Why, one winter, there was a veritable invasion. I was forced—"

"Stop. Just stop. You remove dead mice from the house? Did I hear you correctly? Oh gosh, listen to me. I'm talking to my own imaginary figment as if he's real."

"Please sit," the bearded man said. "Give yourself a chance to breathe. It's said that deep breaths help quell the agitated mind."

Hope stared.

"If you're going to faint, it is best to be seated. And, it would make sense to put aside the glass."

"If I sit, will you go away?"

The ghost sighed. "Try it and find out."

Hope returned to her chair and sat. Then, she carefully placed the wine glass on the table, suddenly happy that it hadn't broken on the carpet. That would have created a bigger mess, which she didn't need. She told herself to be calm, close her eyes, and count to ten. She thought that ten would be long enough. In a way, she was thankful for the wine. The alcohol might be the only thing that kept her from becoming hysterical. After all, her unknown disease was accelerating at full speed.

At the end of ten counts, Hope opened her eyes.

No one stood by the window. She breathed a sigh of relief.

"Do you feel better?"

Hope turned. The bearded man stood to one side of the room.

"No," Hope said as her heart sank. "I don't."

"If you would permit me a bit of logic," the bearded man said. "Let's examine what is happening. We both know you've checked the locks and doors and windows of this house repeatedly, and you've found no breach, correct?"

"That doesn't mean much." Hope's voice sounded tiny.

"It means that there is no way I could have entered the premises without breaking in. So, I can't be a living person. I'm a person, but I no longer have a corporeal body. In other words, I am a spirit. That seems perfectly in keeping with the known facts."

"Or you might have been conjured up by my addled brain," Hope suggested.

"That's a valid conclusion, but do you really think you could conjure up someone as complete as me? I mean, I do sound like a regular fellow, don't I?"

"I have a very good imagination. I believe I could imagine someone like you."

"So, if I disappear and reappear, it won't change your mind, will it? Since you can see yourself inventing such a trick?"

"I'm more than capable of such a thing," Hope said weakly.

"I'm sure you are. But are you capable of mussing up your purse, or dropping a dead mouse here and there?"

"I suppose I could imagine...."

"The mice were real. Even your daughter knows that."

Hope paused to think. The bearded man was

right about that. Cori had found the first mouse and even disposed of it. That really happened, Hope hadn't imagined that.

"My brain is using that fact to bolster your case," Hope said. "Nothing more."

"This is not going the way I'd hoped. What will it take to convince you?"

"I suppose any trick I dream up will simply be an add-on to my hallucination. So, I'm not sure there is anything you can do."

The bearded man frowned. "What if I tell you something that you don't already know?"

"It might be just another detail I make up."

"Unless, there is a way to verify the detail. After all, you can't make up what you don't know. And if what I tell you is true, then, I must be real. Does that make sense?"

"In a way," Hope said warily. "I suppose that verifying what you tell me is some sort of proof."

"Exactly." The bearded man paced back and forth. "The trick is to tell you something that you couldn't possibly know and yet offer you a way to verify it. Not as simple as one would suppose. Let me try this. At one time, I owned several ships that hauled cotton out of the port of Wilmington. They traveled to various ports. Do you have any idea what the names of my ships were?"

Hope thought a moment. "I have no idea."

"Exactly. And I owned a cotton plantation in South Carolina. Do you know the name of my plantation?"

"No."

"So, here are the facts that you don't know, but can verify. My ships were named Alice, for my wife, Jewel, for my daughter, and Euphemia, for my mother. My plantation was named Tarden Hall, after the Tarden family, the original owners. I believe you can verify all of these facts. If you made up the names, then, of course, you won't be able to verify them."

"Unless, I somehow know your history."

"True. So, let me offer this. Before you do your research, talk to your daughter. See if she remembers any of the names, or even your interest in the builder of this house. I think you may put trust in her answers."

Hope thought for a moment. The plan seemed sound, but she wasn't at all sure she would carry it out. No, she was sure she would. Seeking the answers would not only say something about this figment, but would also prove the existence of a serious mental issue she was suffering from. If she didn't have a physical ailment, she certainly had a need for a therapist. She didn't know which was worse, since she couldn't afford either one.

"All right," Hope said. "I feel silly, but I'll look for the proof of your existence. And let's say I find it. What then?"

"Then, I wish to speak with you concerning a task I would trust to your efforts."

"A task? What sort of task?" Hope looked at the ghost with a questioning expression.

"I will leave that until the next time we speak. It strikes me as premature to name the task before we have come to trust one another."

"You want me to trust a ghost?"

"In a word, yes. I think you will find me an honorable man. Our dealings will be strictly consensual. And now, I'm going to disappear. I say that in order to warn you, lest you take the opportunity to faint."

"Wait," she said. "When will I speak with you again?" Hope rolled her eyes. She was speaking to a non-entity as if it were real.

"I would like to chat with you again tomorrow night. I hope that will give you sufficient time to do whatever it is you need to do."

"Sure, whatever, same time, same place."

"Very good."

"Tomorrow is certainly a good time to guarantee that I'm bonkers."

Before her eyes, the bearded man ceased to be. He was gone in the blink of an eye.

"Wait," Hope called. "What were those names again?"

The voice came from the empty air. "Alice, Jewel, Euphemia, Tarden Hall."

Hope grabbed a pen and scribbled down the names, even though she thought it was ridiculous. Yet, she was intrigued enough to tackle the list—the next day. She was in no condition to do the verification right then. The morning would be soon enough, more than soon enough. And she knew she had to keep this entire psychotic episode to herself. If she started telling people about the ghost in the attic, she would lose her teaching job and probably her daughter. Ghosts were best reserved for therapists and maybe, not even them. Some secrets were taken to the grave, weren't they?

Hope gathered her glass and turned off the lights and returned to the first floor, where she told Cori it was time for bed.

"By the way," Hope said. "You haven't found any

more dead mice around, have you?"

"No, that would be icky," Cori said.

"Exactly." Hope wanted to ask if Cori had heard any voices in the house, but that seemed like a step too far. What would Cori think if she started asking questions about spirits and ghosts?

In bed, Hope made an effort to quiet her mind. The same question roiled around inside her head. Just how bad was her health issue? How debilitating would it become? How long did she have before she started seeing angels and telling people she was the reincarnation of Catherine the Great? If she looked on the bright side, thinking she was Catherine the Great might be a boon. People would take care of her then, right? No more worries? She sighed heavily.

Sleep came late, and the morning came early.

Hope remembered with dread what had happened in the attic office, and she purposefully avoided thinking about it. The list of names was on the table ... the list she didn't want to read or process. She settled in the kitchen with her coffee and laptop computer. She didn't want to give any credence to what had happened the night before. It was a memory she wished she could erase. Maybe she could. Maybe it really didn't happen.

What if there isn't any list?

The question bounced around inside her head. What if there was nothing but a blank sheet of paper? No words? No names? Had she traveled so far down the road to insanity that she'd only thought she had written down the names? And now, she was too frightened to go and look. What was wrong with her?

"Hey, Mom."

Hope turned to Cori. What might happen when Hope stopped recognizing her daughter?

"I have a job for you," Hope said.

"Can't I eat breakfast first?"

"You can do this while you eat breakfast."

"That helps."

"And it's easy, it's what you do every day."

"Eat?" Cori asked with a smile.

"Funny. I want you to do some research for me."

"Maximillian Johnson?"

"How did you know?"

"You mentioned it already."

"Good. But I want you to come up with some specific answers."

Cori raised her eyebrows.

"It's my understanding," Hope said, "that Maximillian had ships and a cotton plantation. I want you to come up with the names of those things."

"Names?"

"Yes, names of the ships and the plantation. See, I told you it would be easy."

Hope got ready to head out.

"And what will you do?" Cori asked.

"Laundry. Want to trade?"

Cori laughed. "Not a chance."

The laundry was done by noon. The cake had to be delivered by three, which was the time of the wedding. The reception was slated for four-thirty, which was fine with Hope. She found Cori in her room.

"Time to shower," Hope said. "We have to deliver a cake."

"I found the names."

Anxiety rushed through Hope's veins as she stared at her daughter.

"The names of Max Johnson's ships and plantation. Don't you want the information now? Are you saying I did all this work for nothing?"

"I'm sure it wasn't a whole lot of work, unless you're counting keystrokes or something."

"Funny. But it wasn't as easy as you might think. It wasn't as if he was a major shipper around here."

Hope thought she heard a "thump" up in the attic, but she chased that thought from her mind.

"All right," Hope said. "What are the magic names?"

"The ships were named Jewel, Euphemia, and Alice. The plantation was called Tarden Hall. And those are some weird names."

Hope said, "Thanks a bunch for finding out the information. Now, you need to shower and dress. We can't be late."

When Hope left Cori's room, her hands were trembling. Now, she had to verify those names. She had to go to the attic office and look at the list she was pretty sure she wrote.

She didn't want to verify anything, but she had to do something. She needed to know just how far down the rabbit hole she'd fallen. She trudged up to the attic and made sure she was seated before she picked up the pad she'd written on.

Alice, Jewel, Euphemia, Tarden Hall.

Hope bit her lip. The names were the same, and she hadn't cheated in any way. Panic nibbled at her brain. She tried to fashion an explanation that would make use of all the specifics. What if she had somehow communicated the names to Cori via a mind meld, like in Star Trek. Mothers and daughters were said to enjoy a special bond, a special way of communicating. That made sense. She had implanted the names by mind control. Hope groaned at her wild explanation.

But that didn't explain Cori's online search.

Perhaps, just perhaps, the reverse happened. Cori had relayed the names to Hope as they popped up on the screen. That made sense.

But if that was how it happened, when had Hope written down the names? She hadn't been in the office all day. She was pretty sure she hadn't been in the office all day. She didn't remember being in the office. But if her brain wasn't working properly, would she remember going to the office? She didn't think so.

"Satisfied?"

The voice no longer made her jump, but it did startle her. She turned to where the bearded man stood.

"Hardly," she said. "But I have to admit, it's a neat trick."

"It's no trick, but it is a start. If you can bring yourself to chat with me on a regular basis, I believe we will both become accustomed to our different existences."

Hope thought for a moment. "I guess so. Why

not?" she said. "I may as well enjoy my trip into my mind-forged fantasy."

"I hope that as we talk more, you will come to realize that you have not invented me, as I have not invented you."

"That might be easier to believe. I'm a figment of your imagination. I never considered that."

"Please, let us not indulge in useless prattle. I wish to use your skills and services."

"I wish I could help," she said. "But right now, I have a gig to work."

"Gig? You mean like gigging a frog?"

Hope chuckled. "No, nothing like that. A gig is a job, a short job, mostly a one-day job."

"That's a rather odd use of the word."

"Exactly, but words change over time, as I'm sure you understand."

"I hope to learn more, but for now, I will leave you to your 'gig.' When will you return?"

"Does it matter? I would think a ghost like you would have no need for time."

"It's strange that you would think time stops just because one is dead. While we might have little need for clocks, we certainly are subject to time, as are all creatures. Time and tide wait for no man."

"Or woman." Hope stood. "I should be back by evening."

"I will await your return with bated breath."

Right before Hope's eyes, the bearded man faded to nothing. As she stared at the wall, she thought to herself that no one used the phrase "bated breath" anymore. Then, she told herself that her brain might be up to the task of equipping her figment with appropriate language. That would be something. She had never heard of anyone imagining another person with customized language. If she weren't so worried about her brain, she might have laughed.

14

Edsel smiled when Hope ushered Cori into the bakery.

"My, my," Edsel said. "Don't you two look nice. You're all dressed up for the wedding."

"We're just going to the reception," Cori said.

"The reception," Edsel corrected herself. "Well, you two will outshine the bride ... which is never a good thing."

"We will hardly outshine anyone," Hope said. "But you're very kind to say so."

With Cori's help, Hope managed to move the wedding cake from the cooler to the back of her SUV. She was tempted to put Cori in with the box, to keep it from toppling over, but that would leave Cori out of a seatbelt, and that would be dangerous.

So, Hope drove very, very slowly to the country club. She and Cori carried the cake to the ballroom, thankful that the club had an elevator. They unboxed and placed the cake in the center of a long table that held the two plates, two goblets, a knife, two forks, and two of everything the bride and groom would need. Everything was silver and shiny, the way the wedding planner wanted it.

"The cake is absolutely perfect," the wedding planner gushed. She was about Hope's age but thinner and wearing black-rimmed glasses that made her look bookish. In a tan dress, the wedding planner was not going to turn heads, which was her intent. Wedding planners who stole the show didn't get a lot of work, no matter how successful the wedding was. Would-be brides and their mothers hired the wedding planner to remain in the background.

"I have to get back to the church," the wedding planner said. "You can never trust the photographer or videographer to do their jobs right. They'll probably get the scaffolding in the background, which would ruin everything."

"Scaffolds?" Hope asked.

"The church is scheduled for a refurbishment, and there are stacks of scaffolds in the side chapel.

The wedding is the last event scheduled, and the bride's mother is the only reason the church is still open. You've met her, so you understand. Hang around, get something to drink. Everyone will arrive within the hour."

Hope thought that if the wedding planner couldn't trust the people she hired, then the wedding planner needed to hire other people. Still, Hope and Cori grabbed two soft drinks and sat at a table in the rear. Waiting wasn't Hope's strong suit. Cori was better off, as she had brought her phone.

"What is happening in the twitter world?" Hope asked.

"You should join it and find out," Cori answered.

"No, thanks. You can tell me what I need to know."

Cori made a face. "Well, in the twitter world, there is some talk about Dad."

Hope's smile faded. "There is? What does it say?"

"Well, it's not an *it*. It's a *reporter* back in Ohio, who said the accident looks suspicious."

"Suspicious, how?"

Cori rolled her eyes and handed over her phone. "Why don't you read it. I have to use the restroom."

Hope took the phone and frowned at the tiny

print. How could Cori read this? She stared and read, and what she read made her stomach clench.

The reporter had reviewed the police reports and questioned how there could be a one-car crash on a perfectly straight, dry highway, in the middle of the afternoon, where the driver had no alcohol or drugs in his system. It didn't make sense, unless the driver committed suicide, and the reporter didn't find any evidence of that. Hope was both upset and thankful at the same time. She held the same doubts in her mind, and she had come to the same conclusion.

Doug didn't want to die. He hadn't killed himself. But what *had* happened? Was he on his phone? Was he distracted? Was that the reason he'd died that day? What was the logical answer?

Of course, she told herself that she no longer needed to be logical, not after chatting with a hundred-year-old ghost. She shook her head. What was she going to do with her addled brain?

Soon the wedding guests arrived and took seats at their assigned tables. Hope and Cori stayed at the back. The guests were well-dressed and they immediately went to the corner bars for the alcohol that would allow them to stay in their seats for the next few hours. A reception without alcohol was generally a short affair.

The wedding party arrived and were announced by the emcee. Hope remembered when receptions didn't have emcees or announcements. Did anyone really care that the best man was nick-named "Sparky," or the maid of honor was the girl "most likely to" in the high school yearbook? To Hope, it seemed as if the emphasis had left the bride and groom, and had settled on the entourage. She had the idea that, sooner or later, weddings would revert to more simple celebra-tions. A short ceremony, a small reception, and a race to a car decorated by the best man and maid of honor. Those were the events she would enjoy baking for.

Hope and Cori waited through the usual rounds of bawdy jokes and innuendos. The best man, who admitted to dating the bride before the groom stole her away, gave a rather sheepish toast. He didn't sound too terribly happy at the turn of events, but he did manage to end the toast with the appropriate wish for happiness to shower the newly married couple.

The maid of honor followed with her own version of the toast. While she had no relationship with the groom, she did gloss over a spring vacation in Mexico, which she and the bride remembered.

The crowd laughed, and then it was time for the cutting of the cake and the toast of champagne.

Hope didn't know who invented the custom of force-feeding cake to one's spouse, but with laughter, the groom smushed some cake into the bride's mouth, and she returned the favor. Everyone laughed, although neither bride nor groom looked terribly pleased.

The groom looked positively stricken.

That was when Hope looked at him with concern.

The groom frowned, grabbed his throat, and then looked down at his chest. A moment later he collapsed, the bride staring with a look of disbelief.

It was the best man who rushed forward and knelt beside the fallen groom. He looked up and shouted, "Someone call 911."

That was when Hope heard Cori speaking into her phone.

"The country club," Cori said. "Yes, I'll stay on the line."

15

Hope's desire to leave the reception immediately after the cake cutting was dashed by the collapse of the groom. In fact, no one was allowed to leave. Everyone had to watch the EMTs rush in and try to revive the fallen young man. Everyone had to wait until the police had taken names and addresses. There were too many people to process. The wedding party was asked to stay, along with the wedding planner, and Hope, the baker of the cake that seemed to be responsible for the groom's misfortune.

Everyone had seen the groom consume the cake and immediately keel over. Conclusions were jumped to in seconds. A fast-acting poison was the reason of choice, or perhaps an allergic reaction.

Most people had watched too many TV shows. And now, many of them were giving Hope accusatory looks.

A handsome black man slid onto a chair across from Hope and Cori and smiled. The man was in his early forties with close-cropped hair and straight, white teeth. He was tall and slender and looked good in his tan, summer suit, which seemed just right for a wedding. Too many people wore dark colors to weddings as if it were some sort of funeral.

"I'm Detective Derrick Robinson," the man said, "with the Castle Park police, and if you have a minute, I'd like to ask a few questions."

"We have no place to be," Hope said. "But we would like to get out of here."

"Me, too." He held up a phone. "Do you mind if I record this?"

"Not at all," Hope said.

"I want an attorney," Cori said crossing her arms over her chest.

"What?" Derrick asked.

"She's kidding," Hope said.

"No, I'm not," Cori said. "The first rule of the Twitterverse is never talk to police without an attorney present."

"I thought it was immunity," Derrick said. "You're supposed to get immunity."

Cori stared. "You use Twitter?"

"Who doesn't?"

Cori pointed to Hope. "She doesn't."

Hope felt Derrick's stare, and she shrugged. "I find it very difficult to distill a thoughtful statement into a hundred characters."

"One hundred and forty," Cori corrected.

"So much more," Hope mocked.

"Two problems," Derrick said to Cori. "One, you're a minor and therefore, not eligible for immunity or an attorney, unless your parents say so. Two, your..." Derrick looked at Hope.

"Mother," Hope provided.

"Mother has not asked for an attorney, but then, she's not under arrest, so an attorney would be only a large expense, as attorneys don't come cheap."

"You can record us," Hope said with a smile. "Especially, if it will speed up the process. I hope we don't have to spend the night answering questions."

Derrick set the phone on the table. "All right, for the record, this is Detective Derrick Robinson with..."

"Hope Herring."

He looked at Cori.

"Cori Herring, under protest," Cori said.

Hope listened as the detective read off the time and date for the "record." She knew that such details were necessary, as no one's memory was like a recording. Details were always being lost or found long after the fact.

"If my information is correct," Derrick said. "You are the baker who made the cake."

"That is correct," Hope said. "And I used nothing but natural ingredients and some dye. So, the cake couldn't have caused the collapse."

"And no one could have tampered with the cake?"

"Well, it was kept in the cooler at the bakery, so I suppose someone might have had the opportunity to tamper with it."

"The Butter Up Bakery?"

"Yes, Edsel Morgan owns it, and she hired me as her cake baker. I do all sorts of cakes, including wedding cakes and cupcakes."

"Great, but you didn't see anyone tamper with the cake?"

"No, but I'll point out now, and I'm sure you're aware, I don't know of a single poison that acts as quickly as the groom collapsed. That is the stuff of

TV crime shows. And since the bride didn't collapse, I'd conclude that the cake is perfectly fine."

"Unless it was an allergic reaction," Derrick said. "The bride might not share the same allergy as the groom."

"Even an allergic reaction takes some time. People don't just instantly drop to the ground."

"I agree, but the crime team is still taking samples from the cake."

"I think it's a waste of time, but I understand that it's necessary."

"My mother would never put anything dangerous in a cake," Cori said.

"I thought you were going to be mum," Hope said.

Cori looked stricken. "I am."

The detective went on to ask some routine questions about Hope's relationship to the groom, bride, families, and even the wedding planner. Hope reported that she had no relationship to anyone associated with the wedding, with the exceptions of the wedding planner and the mother of the bride, whom Hope had met once.

"We've just moved here from Ohio," Hope said. "I don't know many people here in Castle Park."

"You bought the Johnson house, right?" Derrick asked.

"I did," Hope answered.

"How do you like the ghost?"

"Ghost?" Hope blinked fast. "What ghost?"

Derrick gave Hope a smile. "The one that's supposed to be in the house. I've never seen it, but according to the kids I went to school with, there's a ghost living in the attic. But then, the house has stood vacant more often than it's had occupants. So, ghost stories are bound to crop up."

"Well, I can assure you that there are no ghosts in the house," Hope said. "At least, none so far." She wasn't about to admit to seeing a ghost, as that might constitute grounds for separating her from Cori. Hope wasn't going to do anything that would call her mothering abilities into question.

There were a few more questions and then the detective said, "Well, that wraps this up." Derrick turned off the phone. "Unless something else pops up, I see no reason for you to hold out for immunity." He grinned. "No matter what the Twitterverse says."

"Are we free to go?" Hope asked.

"Yes, ma'am. If I need more information, I'll be in touch."

"When you get the coroner's report," Hope asked, "can you share it with me?"

"Why would you be interested in it?"

"I'd like proof that there was nothing in or on the cake that caused a problem. It would be good to know that. If people start thinking the cake was poisoned, then I won't get many customers."

He chuckled. "I see your point. So, yes, if the cake is exonerated, I'll let you know."

They all stood, the detective thanked them, nodded, and moved off. Hope herded Cori toward the exit.

"I don't like him," Cori said.

"Why not?" Hope asked.

"He didn't let me get an attorney, and he didn't read us those rights they say on TV."

"We weren't under arrest. He had no reason to make us aware of our Miranda rights."

"That's no excuse."

"It is for a policeman."

"Well, next time, I want immunity."

"I'm sure you'll get it.

The wedding planner stood outside the front door smoking a cigarette and as Hope passed by, the woman exhaled a large cloud of smoke into the air.

"Oh. Excuse me," the wedding planner said.

Hope turned.

"There wasn't anything in the cake, right?" the wedding planner asked. "I wouldn't ask, but the groom dropped right after eating a bite of it."

Hope said, "I doubt the cake had anything to do with anything since the bride seems to be in perfectly good shape."

"That makes sense." The wedding planner nodded. "I just want you to know that I'm still going to use Butter Up for my cakes."

"Thanks. I appreciate that. Somebody should probably check the champagne though."

The wedding planner stared, and then laughed. "Right, as if someone could poison a champagne bottle."

"Not the bottle, just the glass."

With that, Hope pushed Cori toward their SUV.

16

"Do you really think someone poisoned the champagne?" Cori asked.

"No, not really. First, we don't know that it was poison that caused the death. It might have been a heart attack."

"He was pretty young for a heart attack."

"The funny thing about heart attacks is that they can happen at any age, especially if someone is doing drugs. Remember that the next time someone offers you a pill or something."

"No one has ever offered me a pill," Cori said with a shake of her head. "And I don't think anyone is ever going to."

"Someone probably will, and that someone will

encourage you to take it. Don't do it. That would be stupid."

"And I'm not stupid, right?"

"Not yet." Hope chuckled.

"Ha, ha," Cori mocked. "What's for dinner?"

"Not cake," Hope said. "How about fried chicken?"

"Works for me."

Hope finished changing into her pajamas before she had dinner with Cori. Then, she did a bit of extra cleaning, trying to find things to do, avoiding the trek to the office in the attic, where her brain apparently didn't work so well. In time, she ran out of busy work and trudged up the steps.

She would have liked to avoid the office completely, yet, she couldn't bring herself to stop climbing the stairs. There were things about her affliction that she simply had to explore. Was she really losing her mind?

Hope sat at her computer and waited.

Nothing happened.

For a moment, she wondered where the ghost was, but only for a moment. Then, with a sigh, she opened up her browser and searched for the news item she'd read on Cori's phone. What had the reporter really said about her husband's death? Had the reporter written other articles about the crash? Hope needed to know all she could.

"How was the wedding?" the ghost asked.

Hope was startled out of her concentration. "Nope," she said out loud. "I did not hear that."

"But you did," the man said. "And denying it doesn't make any sense. Are you in the habit of denying what must be the truth?"

Hope turned, and there stood the bearded man, leaning against the wall, looking exactly the same as before.

"I have never and will never deny the truth," Hope said. "Which is why I believe my brain has become diseased to the point that it has invented you. And don't you ever change clothes?"

"What need do I have of clothes? And I'll have you know that this was my best suit, the one they buried me in. In my world, there are no other clothes."

"I'll have to speak to my brain. I'm certain I can come up with some sort of updated wardrobe."

"This is not going as well as I had hoped, Mrs. Herring, but I shall endure. I have waited a very long time for justice, and I am prepared to wait longer. But for now, how was the wedding?"

"You don't know?"

"How would I know? I exist in this house, and this house only. So, I have no knowledge of anything that happens outside this house. Oh, there are other ghosts in other places that I might be able to contact, but I have no need. And they, anchored as they are to their own places, are not privy to a lot of information."

"Anchored?" Hope asked. "That happens to ghosts?"

"It is the only way to remain," the bearded man said. "Otherwise, we are all gathered up and removed. I don't know all the details, as I have decided to stay, but it's my understanding that once gathered up and moved, other processes take place. The only way to know of those things is to experience them. I have no reason to go that route ... yet."

"Why not? Why are you hanging around? Although since I made you up, I guess I should know why you're still here."

"Isn't it obvious? I'm here to obtain justice."

"Justice? What sort of justice does a ghost need?"

"The kind that will allow me to rest in peace and move on. It's not as if I don't want to cross over. I simply can't allow it until I get justice."

Hope shook her head. "But justice for what?"

"In case you have not been informed," the

bearded man said. "I was murdered, here, in my own home. I wish to have justice for my murder."

"Why? Don't you know who killed you?"

The bearded man rolled his eyes. "Listen closely. If I knew who killed me, why would I seek justice? I would have exacted justice from the miscreant long before now. I would have moved on."

"You're a ghost, and you don't know how you died?!" Hope couldn't keep the confusion out of her voice.

"Of course, I know *how* I died. I simply do not know *who* killed me. Why is that so hard to believe?"

"I always thought that death was the great revelation. That you learned all there was to learn once you passed on."

"Precisely, Mrs. Herring, you learn everything once you've moved on. I have not moved on, hence, I have not learned what so many of us want to learn. And once I have moved on, I will not be in any position to ensure justice has been served. Are you beginning to see my predicament?"

Hope rubbed her forehead. Talking to her illusion was beginning to give her a headache. And why was she talking in the first place? If he came from her brain, she merely had to think her answers, not say them.

"I understand and can appreciate the problem I present," the bearded man said. "After all, I never met a ghost while I was alive. If one had tried to contact me, I would have questioned my own soundness of mind. I ask only that you give yourself a chance to understand. Give yourself the permission to believe, if only for as long as it takes to solve my murder."

"Solve your murder? Is that what this is about?" Hope's eyes were wide.

"I would think that was obvious. What other justice could I wish for?"

Hope shrugged.

"A person must have a powerful goal if one is to forego crossing to the other side. The solution to my murder is such a goal."

Hope asked, "Can't you go back in time or something and simply watch what happened to you?"

The bearded man massaged his temples, as if he were developing a headache. "Let us assume, if only for the moment, that I have pursued each and every path I could imagine in order to achieve my goal. No, I cannot travel in time, although that would certainly be beneficial. No, I cannot leave this house, which would be another boon. My only hope to reach my sworn result is to enlist help ... from the living. As I explained, the other dead cannot help me."

Hope sighed in frustration. "How do you think I can help? Your death occurred, what, a hundred years ago?"

"One hundred years, one month, and twelve days, to be exact." The bearded man smiled. "And, yes, I keep count."

Hope glanced at her computer screen. "I need to go," she said.

"When will you return?" he asked. "I wish to settle on the details and terms of your investigation."

"Terms?"

"I can hardly expect you to work for nothing," he said. "While I have very little to offer, I can, perhaps, provide some support."

Hope shook her head. It was far past the time where she could think straight. "We'll ... I'll think about this. I need some time to get used to what's happening."

"Please, give it a deep perusal," the bearded man said. "While my thirst for justice is great, I have been seeking it for a long time. I need to achieve my goal and move on. I'm certain you agree."

With that, the bearded man disappeared.

Hope glanced at her computer, and while she

might have wanted to read more articles about her husband's death, she knew she couldn't do it in the office. Grabbing her laptop, she left and went downstairs to the kitchen. She supposed that the bearded man could find her there, yet, she hoped she would not be hounded in her own kitchen.

Looking around once, she opened her browser and continued with the search she had started in the attic. She needed to learn all she could about Doug's death.

Later as Hope tried to sleep, she had a sudden, discomforting thought. If the bearded man could come and go anywhere in the house, what kept him out of her bedroom? Or Cori's bedroom? The thought left her cold. Not that she had come to believe in the bearded man. It was just that the thought of his existence raised major problems. Perhaps, she could program her brain not to allow him in the bedrooms. Was that possible? She fell asleep before she could figure out how that might occur.

Sunday meant church, but Hope had not yet decided on a church to join. She was a believer of sorts, and she wanted to expand her circle of friends. Coming to a brand-new town required some outreach on her part, especially since she was going to be a teacher in the community school. She knew she would meet parents, but she wanted to meet people who didn't have children in school.

She and Cori spent Sunday doing outdoor tasks. She wanted the house and grounds to look as good as possible.

Hope managed to avoid the attic office until after dinner. She might have liked to avoid it altogether, but she needed to talk to her "ghost." She felt terribly odd as she walked up the stairs to the attic. She was beginning to believe that she might not be ill and that the ghost could be real. She needed to chat with the spirit, Maximillian Johnson.

17

Sitting down to the computer, Hope noticed the names she had written ... Alice, Jewel, Euphemia, Tarden Hall. Those things were real, had been real. She worried for a moment that as a social studies teacher, she might have come across those names at one time or another, but she decided that couldn't be the case. Hope knew she'd never known those names until Max Johnson had said them to her.

"I hope I am not intruding," the ghost said.

Hope turned to the bearded man. "No, you're right on time. And since I'm beginning to believe in you, let's talk about the task you want to hire me for."

Maximillian smiled. "You are a courageous and

wonderful woman. I am lucky to have you on my side."

"I'm not on your side yet. We haven't set down the details of our arrangement. In order to do that, I need to know where you can go, both inside and outside the house."

"As I informed you, I must remain in the house until I'm ready to cross. While going out of the house can be done, it is far too risky. So, I am stuck inside."

"You have complete run of the house?"

"Yes, I can visit whichever room I want."

"I'd like you to avoid my bedroom and the bedroom of my daughter."

"I am not some sort of voyeur. I am perfectly aware of and devoted to your privacy."

"I don't know enough about you to render a judgment about your habits. I'm just making the request. Since I can't keep you out by lock and key, I must take your word that you will not enter the bedrooms unless invited to do so. Is that agreeable?"

"It is most agreeable. Upon my word as a gentle-man, I will not enter the bedrooms unless asked to do so."

"Thank you. I don't want my daughter or my neighbors to know you're here. There are some people who would try to take away my daughter if they heard me talking to a ghost. Do you understand?"

"Indeed, I do. When I was still alive, those who spoke to ghosts were considered unstable."

"Exactly. So, we'll meet here in this office when we need to talk. It doesn't have to be every day, but you are welcome to join me, if I am alone. Is that fair?"

"I can go about the house, except for the bedrooms. I can converse with you only here."

"You got it. And since we're going to work together, my name is Hope."

"I am Maximillian Johnson. You may call me Max."

"What was your wife's name?"

"Alice, and my daughter was Jewel, as I informed you before."

"Were they here when you died?"

"No, they were visiting her parents in Charleston. I was alone at the time of the attack."

"That makes it easier, but I have to tell you that solving a century-old murder mystery won't be simple. It could take a long time and I might not be able to do it."

"I understand."

"Can you write?" Hope asked.

"I assure you that I learned to read and write as a child."

"I assumed you know how. I just mean are you, as a ghost, able to take a pen in hand and write out the names of all your enemies. Of course, they're all dead now, but I need a place to start. A list of possible suspects would be appreciated."

"Of course, how clumsy of me. I shall write out their names, with a brief description, forthwith. And don't think I haven't thought of them every day for the last century. It is virtually all I've thought about."

"You mentioned some sort of payment for my services. What did you mean by that?"

The bearded man frowned. "I have considered remuneration," he said, "and I'm afraid I have little to offer. I have no money, and this house is yours, according to the laws of the land. I have no assets or income. What I can offer is protection."

"Protection? What sort of protection?"

"Total protection against any burglar or thief that might break into the house. Since I do not sleep, I can make sure your sleep is free from worry."

Hope thought a moment. "What would you do if some thief did break in?"

"I am not without some powers. I can trip and hurl objects and perhaps cudgel a thief, if need be. Making myself invisible to the human eye is a benefit under such circumstances."

"Okay, that sounds very good."

"I am at your service, madam. If I find other ways to pay for your time and effort, I will certainly offer them."

"Great. Now, what do you remember about the murder?"

"Please call me Max, and I don't remember a great deal. As you are aware, I did have a small shipping company in Wilmington, not far from here. Since my family was in Charleston, I had ridden my horse into Wilmington. I returned home after dark, which I had often done in the past. I left my horse at the stable I used and walked the rest of the way to the house. There are no more stables, are there? I have not heard the clip-clop of horses' hooves in a long time."

"There are no stables," Hope said. "Just roads and cars."

"I've seen cars, but they baffle me. I cannot fathom how they move without the aid of horse or ox."

Hope nodded. "Go on with the story."

"In those days, we were not accustomed to lock our doors while we were away. We reasoned that if someone wanted to get in while we were gone, they would break in if the doors were locked. Of course, we locked the doors while we were at home. That seemed prudent."

"Max," Hope said. "When you returned home, you had no idea if someone was in the house?"

"You are correct. I didn't know that someone was waiting for me. There were no indications that someone had entered the house. The dining room had not been raided for its silver, and my office had not been ransacked."

"Then the motive wasn't theft."

"It would appear not, although Castle Park did have its share of thieves and ne'er-do-wells. Most of those people were not killers. They simply didn't like to work."

"Where did the attack happen?" Hope asked.

Max frowned and then shrugged. "In the kitchen. I was stoking the fire in the stove as I wanted to make coffee. Someone hit me in the back of the head and I blacked out. I lay bleeding in the kitchen for the better part of two days before our thrice-week maid arrived. I didn't learn that until later, as I never regained consciousness. By the time the doctor arrived, I was dead."

"Which is why you never saw your assailant. Had you died immediately, you would have seen him or her?"

"You possess a keen sense," Max said. "You have it right."

"The police investigated, but at the time, forensic clues were rarely taken into account."

"Forensic?"

"Fingerprints, DNA, things that pinpoint a person's physical attributes and genetic material. Hair, skin cells, whatever clues the killer had left behind."

"I don't know about those things. The police visited the house and the kitchen several times, but they did not find clues that led them to the killer."

Hope studied Max for a moment. "They found nothing, and since that time, the house has been made over many times."

"I'm afraid so. The kitchen is nothing like it was when I was killed."

"So, there are no clues to look for." Hope shook her head.

"I'm afraid not. The only room that hasn't been changed or at least cleaned is the rebel hole by the fireplace."

"Rebel hole?" Hope asked. "What's that?"

"Are you familiar with the priest holes once popular in Europe?"

"A place where someone could hide without being detected?"

"Yes, well, after the war of northern aggression...."

"The Civil War," Hope corrected.

"Call it what you will, the South did not invade the North, and our armies did not march across New York."

"Let's not fight the war all over. Tell me about a rebel hole."

"As I said, since there were times when a soldier or legislator or notable was being pursued by the winning side, some houses equipped themselves with small spaces where a patriot might hide."

"I see," Hope said. "And you installed such a space?"

"I did, purely as a contingency. No one ever used it. In any case, as you face the fireplace, the button for the door is located on the right side, up against the mantle. It looks like just another berry carved into the oak. Yet, if you press it, the door pops open."

"And it's large enough to hide a man?"

"Two, if they would be willing to crowd each other."

"And no one has ever found this hole?"

"No one."

"I'll have to see about it. Let's get back to the murder. There are no physical clues to be found, so we have to rely on the list of enemies and possible killers, along with your memories. I am not at all certain we're going to solve this case."

"But you must," Max said. "You represent my best and perhaps my last chance to achieve justice."

"Thank you for the vote of confidence, but I can guarantee nothing except some hard work. So, write me that list of possible killers, and if you would, put the one with the best motive at the top."

"Oh, that's easy. That would be Captain Thomas, a cad and a scalawag if ever there was one."

"Okay, good."

"I will make the list." Max disappeared, and Hope stared after him.

For a moment, she wondered what she had gotten herself into, and then, she chuckled. She had gotten herself into a one-way ticket to some institution, if anyone found out she was talking to a ghost.

The next morning, Hope dropped off Cori and proceeded to the bakery. She had no sooner walked through the door when Edsel called out.

"You have to tell me all about the murder," Edsel said. "But I'm pretty sure I know who killed him."

18

"You do?" Hope asked. "How? You need to call the police. Tell them what you know. But tell me first."

"It was his bride. She fed him some cake, and he choked to death. I don't think she ever really loved him to begin with."

"He didn't choke to death," Hope corrected. "In fact, I don't know what killed him. It might have been something completely natural. No one will know until the coroner puts out his report."

"Mark my words. If she didn't kill him, she was involved in some other way."

"Why do you say that?"

"Carter is a spoiled brat. I don't think she loved Randy at all. She likes the idea of *being* in love and having the big wedding and all the trappings. Maybe she figured out it was a mistake to marry him and wanted to get out of it somehow. She and Randy weren't a good match," Edsel said.

After more discussion, Hope said, "Well, I really hope that isn't the case." She shook her head and changed the subject. "What cakes do we have on the schedule today?"

"I put a list on your work table. No wedding cakes, just some for the case and a birthday cake is needed this afternoon."

"You got it, boss."

Edsel rolled her eyes. "Don't call me boss."

"Okay, boss." Hope chuckled all the way back to her work table.

The day passed quickly. Hope made the birthday cake first, as it had to be ready at a certain time. The decorations were not complicated, so she managed it with ease. The other cakes were simple. She even had time for some cupcakes that she thought resembled art. She frosted the cupcakes to look like flowers and they came out beautifully.

Dinner was highlighted by Cori's story about the homeless man whom she found sound asleep in a deep corner of the library. She thought to report him, but since he wasn't bothering anyone, she let it go. Even the homeless needed a place to rest.

After dinner, Hope retreated to her office, where she found an elegantly written list of names.

My dear Mrs. Herring,

Here is the list you requested. I hope it meets your needs. If not, feel free to contact me. You know how.

Captain Jackson Elmo Thomas – The worst of the worst on land, but a gifted leader by sea. Our dispute centered on jetsam he had left behind during a storm. I docked his portion of the profits. He claimed the action saved the boat. The Maritime Commission sided with me.

Charlotte Mae Kendrick – A woman of ill repute who claimed her husband had earned a bonus he had not earned. Her husband had jumped ship in Havana, no doubt to get away from her. A member of the Harridan family, her voice could sandblast a hull.

Mason Paul Sander – A rival for my wife's hand. Mason once swore to get even with me, although I did not set out to steal his betrothed. For us, it was love at first sight, something Mason could never understand.

Noah William Wells – Noah wanted Tarden Hall. He was negotiating when I made inquiries. He was late gathering up backers and hence, lost out on the planta-tion. He did not take it well.

Aiden Allen Berne – Aiden bet foolishly in a poker

game. He lost everything and then accused everyone at the table of cheating. Aiden was a poor card player and couldn't accept that. He left Castle Park, but not before swearing to get back what had been stolen from him. I was but one of five he threatened.

Haley June Watson nee Conrad – Haley lost her husband during a storm that devastated Tarden Hall. I settled with her per the terms of our contract, but she swore she was owed more. Women can make formidable foes.

Preston Lee Conrad – Brother of Haley and as mean as a water moccasin. He promised me that I would rue the day I cheated his sister out of her inheritance. Preston is more bark than bite, but it would not be beyond him to sneak up and slay someone.

Davis Elvon Ellison – Partner for the ship Euphemia, which was lost in a hurricane, along with all hands. We split the insurance, according to our agreement. When I declined to enter into a new agreement, he fired a shot over my head. I would not be cowed. He left the state.

Wyatt Smith Johnson – A cousin who inherited his father's plantation and ran it into the ground. He came to me to borrow an inordinate sum, and I refused. He blamed me for the loss of the plantation. He became a seed seller around Charleston and lived poorly.

Zachariah MacDermott – A Scot who came to Wilm-

ington to make his mark. Offered to let me invest in a fishing boat in Scotland. However, I was unable to verify the existence of the boat and informed the other would-be investors. Zachariah blamed me for the unraveling of his plan.

I hope this list helps in our endeavor. I trust your discretion in all investigations.

Sincerely,

Maximillian Johnson

Hope read the list twice and had no idea where to start. Because she was a social studies teacher, she knew just how difficult it would be to research non-famous people who were dead and gone. Anyone could study Abe Lincoln. Finding information about Captain Thomas would be much more difficult. Hope would have to go through any number of census forms and old newspapers, provided the newspapers and forms still existed. Fire and flood had come and gone, and they were often the enemies of history.

But she knew where to begin.

With Cori.

Since Cori had free time and would be in the library, she could start the tedious job of chasing down individuals who may or may not have made any kind of name for themselves. The search would be long and hard, but she knew her daughter would be up for the challenge. Hope laid down the pages of script and typed the information into a document that she could send to her daughter, with the proper instructions. At first, Cori, would complain, but eventually, she'd become intrigued and would do the work in the end. Hope was sure of that.

The next day, Hope was busy with a birthday cake for a nine-year-old girl named Wednesday. She had no idea why people picked days or months or cities or states for names. Whatever happened to Sally and Jennifer?

The little bell over the bakery door rang and Hope looked up to see Detective Robinson.

19

"I love the smell of a bakery," the detective said. "It always makes me want to eat."

"Then, you've come to the right place," Hope said. "What can I do for you?"

"I told you that when I got the coroner's report I'd stop by."

Hope's face took on a look of worry. "Please tell me that my cake had nothing to do with the death."

"That's correct. The victim was poisoned, but not by your cake. In fact, the coroner said the poison had to have been administered over an hour before the death. That means it was probably consumed right before the ceremony. The champagne they had in the limo couldn't be the source either. Besides, if anyone else ingested the tainted drink, they would have died also."

"Well, it's good to know that it wasn't anything I did." Hope sighed with relief. "Are there any likely suspects?"

"Well, I probably shouldn't tell you, but I checked you out, and discovered you might be able to help."

"Checked me out? How do you mean?" Hope looked wary.

"I called the chief of police from your hometown. He told me you have a very keen mind and that you should have been a detective. He said you're very good at researching information and putting facts together. He said you're persistent and determined." The detective held Hope's eyes. "I'm very sorry about your husband."

After Doug died, Hope threw herself into investigating the circumstances of his death. She read every article she could find, she talked to the emergency personnel who tended to him at the scene, and to the doctor and nurses at the hospital. Hope sat with the chief of police and went over every detail with him. And after all of that, the death was listed as accidental. Deep down, Hope couldn't accept that was the true cause. Was the *accident* a result of the investigative journalism Doug was doing? Hope thought that was a likely cause.

"Well, the chief was far too complimentary. I didn't do much. I just asked questions."

The detective nodded. "Well, here's what I have so far. Would you mind if I run it past you?"

When Hope nodded, he went on.

"The poison had to have been administered before the ceremony. You know the drill. The best man brings a flask containing liquid courage for the groom. I hate to think of how many grooms didn't back out because they had alcohol in their veins. In any case, I asked the best man about it, and he said sure, they shared a flask. He even handed it over to me. We tested it and found single batch bourbon, some really good stuff, but not poison."

"When did you get the flask?"

"The same night as the murder. And we *are* calling it a murder. No one would believe the groom committed suicide."

"So, the best man offered the flask to you?"

"Not exactly. He brought it out once we asked for it. We still have it."

"There was no other drinking before the ceremony?"

"Not that we could discover. Any ideas?"

"You didn't find a flask on the groom?"

He shook his head. "I thought of that. There was nothing. I checked for an energy drink, you know, something to stoke the fire, so to speak."

"I'm guessing the coroner didn't find any sign of that."

"None. The toxicology screen isn't complete, but the groom wasn't known to do drugs. The coroner found no puncture wounds or other means of administering the poison. Randy must have drunk it. We're stumped."

"So am I, detective. I'm just glad it wasn't the cake."

"Wednesday. What kind of name is that?"

"The modern kind." Hope gave a little shrug.

"I had a great aunt named Euphemia, and I thought that was a weird name."

"Euphemia? Apparently, it was popular at one point in the past. You're the second person I've talked with recently who had a relative with that name."

Derrick made a face. "I don't envy her having that name."

Hope laughed, and Derrick waved as he headed for the door. "If I find out anything else, I'll get back to you."

"Thanks. Good luck."

As Hope turned for the backroom, Edsel put a hand on Hope's arm.

"You're not in trouble, are you?"

"Not one little bit."

"That's good. Cake bakers like you don't come around every day."

"You can thank my mother who taught me a thing or two about sugar."

"I will if she ever comes to visit."

"I'm afraid that won't be happening."

"Oh, I'm very sorry," Edsel said. "There I go sticking my foot in my mouth."

"You had no way of knowing. And it's all right. She had a good life."

"Then, bless her heart."

Cori looked to be in a foul mood when she came down the library steps. Hope wondered if she should ask or just wait. She didn't have to wait long.

"Those names you gave me," Cori said, "don't exist in real life."

"I told you those people lived around a century ago."

"They may have, but that doesn't mean you can find them. Are you sure they existed?"

"I'm pretty sure. Don't worry. You'll find them sooner or later."

"The only one I found was the first one, the captain."

"How did you find him?"

"In a list of sea captains that were lost at sea. How about that? He went down with the ship, or so everyone thought at the time."

"Did you find a reference about him after the sinking of the ship?"

Cori's eyes widened. "How did you know?"

"It wasn't at all uncommon in the old days. A person could move from one state to another and not even have to change his name. There were no social security numbers or drivers' licenses or other forms of identification. Want a new life? Just move."

"Well, this captain didn't change his name. If it's the same man, he went to San Francisco and captained a fishing boat. He may or may not have died in a fight in a local bar."

"You haven't found him in another city?"

"Not yet."

"Keep looking."

"That's easy for you to say."

Despite the heat, Hope enjoyed the walk back to the house. Cori carried the conversation, as she had been talk-starved all day. Will hadn't shown up, for some reason. Text and email were not good substitutes for talk. Hope listened, but she wasn't as interested in the words as in the tone. A happy Cori sounded much different than an unhappy or distracted one. Hope liked to hear the happy Cori.

They passed the church where the unlucky wedding had taken place. The doors were draped in orange construction tape, and Hope remembered hearing that there were scaffolds in the chapel. The refurbishment had begun.

Once they arrived at home, Hope and Cori fixed dinner together which was another special time for Hope. "Bonding" was the psychological term. To Hope, it was just good, old-fashioned "girl talk."

After dinner, Cori went to her bedroom for some chat with the "squad" back in Ohio. Hope knew Cori was still involved with the Ohio teens, and that was to be expected. She was pretty sure that Cori's contact would lessen once school started.

Hope went to her attic office where she sat and looked around, waiting for Max to show up. She didn't have to wait long.

"Good evening, Mrs. Herring," Max said as he appeared by the door.

"Hello," she answered. "Did you have a good day?"

"My days are maddeningly similar. I must sit and wait for you to return with information."

"I have very little, as my daughter has just begun the search. Why didn't you tell me that Captain Thomas was lost at sea?"

"Because he wasn't. The ship was lost, and Jack made it look like he was on the ship, but he wasn't. He turned up in another city. I learned that from another captain who ran into Jack. Apparently, he had neither changed his name nor his penchant for strong liquor. Some men simply cannot keep their mouths closed."

"I take it the good captain lost one of your ships," Hope said.

"Indeed, he scuttled the Euphemia. No one died, as the crew was put into lifeboats. They were certain that Jack had drowned. We were all sure, until he showed up in another port. The man was incorrigible. And he disappeared before I could alert the law to his whereabouts."

"He was indeed a slippery man. Do you think he returned to Castle Park and killed you?"

"The man proved he was capable of anything. I was his nemesis. I posit that I was number one on his list of hated people."

"Perhaps, but there is no proof that he came back

here, but let's say that he did. Where would he go? Where would he stay? Think, Max, where should we look for the footprints he left a century ago?"

Hope watched as Max paced back and forth, his hands behind his back, as he concentrated.

"I know not what structures from long ago survived the years. And I doubt you would be able to find anything about him here. His regular haunts were in Wilmington, from whence he sailed. That would be where I would begin."

"In that case, I need for you to put together a second list."

"Of the places he frequented?"

"Exactly."

"You shall have it in a flash. I cannot thank you enough."

"We have done exactly ... very little," Hope said. "You are no closer to finding your killer than you were decades ago."

"That's not true. For the first time in, well, in more years than I care to count, I have someone on my side. Someone who will chase down my murderer. Don't you see? I have come farther in the last few weeks than I did in a hundred years. That, my dear Mrs. Herring, is progress beyond belief."

"Make the list, Max, and we'll see if we can get a little further along with the case."

"Yes, madam, I will do as you command." Max disappeared.

Hope stared for a moment. She wondered if indeed, her brain was diving down the rabbit hole. But maybe, the ghost *was* real. She wished there was someone else who could see and talk to Max. But who?

It couldn't be an outsider. That might prove dangerous for both her and Max ... especially, if there was no Max. She needed someone she could trust. Her best friends had been left behind in Ohio. She hadn't made that sort of friend yet in Castle Park. Once Hope showed off the ghost, then that other person would have to be sworn to secrecy. Neither of them could go around talking about a ghost or both of them would end up in the asylum.

Hope knew there was really only one person who she could trust, and who would not reveal the secret. One and only one.

Cori.

For a moment, Hope considered if there were any other choices, but there were none. She would have to tell Cori and trust her to guard the secret.

Hope thought it over for a long time, and she

knew the truth of the old adage. When you share a secret with someone, it's no longer a secret. Shaking her head, she knew she couldn't tell her daughter. The best she could do was solve the mystery and send Max on his way.

The next morning, Hope walked Cori to the library where she could research the possible killers of Max, and then, Hope went to Butter Up.

Edsel stood behind the donut case with a hard expression. The person standing in front of the case was the mother of the bride. The woman turned to Hope.

"I want to talk to you," Sandra said.

20

Hope put on her best smile. "What can I do for you?"

"I just wanted you to know that no one blames you for what happened. We all know it wasn't the cake. In fact, the cake was fabulous. I know some ignorant people will think otherwise, but we will not worry about them, will we?"

"Thank you," Hope said. "I appreciate the vote of confidence. How's your daughter?"

"Devastated, as you might guess. If I hadn't seen it myself, I never would have believed it. It's the sort of thing that feeds legends, if you ask me. Luckily, my daughter has her friend, Percy, to lean on. He's been a rock for her."

"Percy, the best man?"

"The very same. Carter and Percy dated for a

while in high school before she found her Randolph. She and Percy have been good friends for years."

"Well, that is lucky," Hope said. "Like you, I've never heard of a groom dying at the reception."

"I'm sure it's happened before, but most grooms with cold feet simply walk away from the church." Sandra smiled. "Oh my, that's not terribly kind, is it? One shouldn't make jokes about the departed. They might come back to haunt you."

"May I ask a question?" Hope said.

"Why, of course you can. What do you want to know?"

"Who was with Percy and Randolph before the ceremony?"

"With them? I don't think anyone was with them. They were out back, hitting on that flask. That's a tried and true tradition here in this area."

"I believe it's common in a lot of places," Hope said. "Liquid courage."

"Oh my, yes. We all need a bit of fortitude on occasion."

Hope watched Sandra leave, and it was only then that Edsel spoke.

"You handled her very well. She isn't at all happy about what happened. She threw a terrific wedding and ended up with no marriage. She's got her lawyer working on the annulment."

Hope said, "I doubt there will be any problem getting the marriage annulled."

"You know, when they were in high school, everyone thought Carter would end up with Percy. They were close. What awful bad luck. I hope it doesn't follow Carter for the rest of her life."

"You can't blame the bride for what happened," Hope said.

"Hon, this is the South. When a girl gets a reputation for bad luck, well, she might not find a husband for a very long while."

Shaking her head, Hope proceeded to the backroom, to her table, and looked at the list of cakes and cupcakes she needed to bake. It was a large order and would keep her busy. That was a good thing.

At lunch, Hope grabbed a salad from the diner and crossed the street to sit on a bench in front of the courthouse. She had just started to eat when Derrick joined her on the bench. He took off his jacket and rolled up his sleeves.

"How are you holding up in the heat?" Derrick asked.

"Just fine," Hope said. "It gets hot in Ohio, too.

J. A. WHITING & NELL MCCARTHY

Maybe, not as humid as here, but it does get humid in the summer there."

"I hear you. Every morning when I wake up, I thank my lucky stars for Willis Carrier."

"Was he the one who invented air conditioning?" Hope asked.

"He was. He did it in Buffalo, New York. Go figure. You would think it would have been someone from the South, where it's always hot."

"Maybe too hot for thinking."

He laughed. "That could be. Have you given any thought to our local murder?"

"I didn't know I was supposed to be thinking about it," Hope said.

"You don't have to, but I think you might like to put your mind to it. Researchers and mystery lovers always come up with the best theories. Not always the right theories perhaps, but good ones in general."

"Well," Hope said, "if you'd like to share what you've learned, I'll listen. Sometimes, simply going over the facts leads to an insight."

"That's a fact, Mrs. Herring, that's a fact. So, I'll tell you what we know. First, the groom, Randy, was poisoned, and he was poisoned some time before the ceremony. We know he and Percy were behind the church, sipping from the flask. We checked the flask. It was clean. Now, Randy might have had something before they got to the church, but no one remembers anything. They came in a limo so it wasn't as if they stopped for a beer or anything."

"I think the most important question is who might have wanted him dead? What are possible motives?"

Derrick took out a handkerchief and mopped his brow. "Not many, according to what we've been able to find out. The groom was well liked, for the most part. There was a young man in college who threatened Randy, but we don't put much in that. Some young men are easily excited and say stupid things on a regular basis."

Hope laughed. "Yes, they do. How about a business associate of Randy's?"

"There is one suspect, an older man with a reputation for violence. He and Randy got into an argument over a used car. It seems the older man accused Randy of not divulging all that should have been divulged in the car sale."

"I'm guessing Randy didn't return any of the man's money."

"Around here, you get a pig in a poke, you deal with it."

"Was the older man around the church on the day of the wedding?"

"He was. He claims he didn't come to cause a problem, but he did talk to Randy. Percy doesn't remember much about the interaction, but he thinks they had a short, serious talk. You know, no hard feelings and all. That doesn't sound like the older man, but who knows. People do strange things sometimes."

"No one else?"

"Well, you think a woman could do it?"

"Poison is a woman's weapon," Hope said.

"I think so, too, and there is one bridesmaid, Heather Allen, who had no love for Randy. Apparently, Heather resented how Randy had treated her younger sister."

"And that's the list of suspects?"

"Pretty short, isn't it?"

"I've seen longer."

"Me, too, and I hate for this killer to get away."

"Suicide is out of the question?"

"Most husbands wait until their first anniversary to kill themselves."

Hope laughed. "And their wives help them."

Derrick smiled widely. "You understand people even better than I do."

"I just have a sense of humor. Well, I have to be getting back to work," Hope said.

"If you have any brainstorms," Derrick said, "feel free to give me a call."

"You'll be the first to know."

Hope walked back to the bakery, thinking about the murder. She had no good theories—except suicide. But there didn't seem to be a reason why Randy would kill himself, especially on such a day, in such a way. The death had to be murder. Hope leaned toward the older man who had been cheated when buying a car. Maybe the longer the old man thought about the bad car deal, the more infuriated he'd become. The old man had dropped by to congratulate the groom? Hope wondered if the old man's purpose in going to the church was to kill Randy and shame him at the same time. What a spectacular way to get revenge.

Cori was in a good mood when Hope went to the library to meet her.

"You look happy," Hope told her daughter as she took a seat at the glossy wood table near the windows.

"I found her."

"You found who?

"Charlotte Mae Kendrick."

Hope thought for a moment and then she recognized the name. She said with excitement, "Oh, you did?"

"I sure did." Cori wore a proud expression.

"That's fantastic. Tell me all about her."

"Don't you want to know how I found her?"

"Sure, fill me in."

"Will started me on the census records, and they're very cool. You can find all sorts of people in old census records. But that's not all. If you know enough, you can find old wedding records and birth records and property records. It's amazing how many records there are for people, and it's not just the rich or famous people. Ordinary people leave a big record track. That's what Will calls it."

"And this record track gave you Charlotte Mae?"

"It did. I don't know everything about her, but she lived in Wilmington part of the time and Castle Park some of the time. There was a newspaper article ... oh, there are newspaper records online, too. Anyway, the article was about her husband, who was lost at sea. Charlotte said he died at sea, but someone else said they saw him in Havana, Cuba, after he supposedly died. So, well, it was a big story, since Charlotte was trying to get money from Maximillian Johnson."

Hope listened as Cori outlined the life and times of Charlotte Mae. It seemed Charlotte Mae had a "colorful" life, working as a seamstress, a tavern barmaid, a landlord, and probably a lady of the night at some point.

Charlotte Mae also raised a stink when Maximillian Johnson didn't pay the insurance her husband took out before he left on Max's ship. There was usually a bounty to be paid if something happened during the voyage. Max was of the opinion that Charlotte Mae and her husband connived to get the money by having him jump ship in Havana. It was an old ploy in the ship business, easy money. Charlotte Mae also married three times—the man who went lost in Havana, another who just went lost, and the third, whom she buried. Cori seemed to get a kick out of the marrying parts.

"Amazing," Hope said, when Cori had finished. "You found out so much."

"And I'm not done," Cori said. "Charlotte Mae disappeared from the area when she was forty-something. I want to know where she went."

"Great. History can be fun, can't it?"

"More fun than I thought."

"Where's your friend, Will?" Hope asked.

"He and his parents were going someplace. He left about an hour ago."

Hope nodded. "I'm going to use the restroom before we head home." She walked through the stacks on her way to the bathroom and stopped short when she heard two people talking on the other side of one of the floor-to-ceiling bookshelves.

"I really despised Randy," a young woman said. "I'm glad he's dead."

Hope's heart began to race.

21

"Oh, Heather. You shouldn't talk like that," another young woman told her.

Hope remembered Derrick telling her that Heather Allen, one of Carter's bridesmaids, was on the suspect list.

"Well, I can't help how I feel. He was awful to my sister. Everyone thinks Randy was so wonderful, but he was selfish and cruel and didn't care about anyone except himself. He didn't deserve to walk this earth." The woman's voice dripped with barely-concealed contempt. "He deserved what he got."

"I thought Carter would be more upset about Randy's death," the other woman said.

Heather replied, "Carter didn't want to marry Randy. She realized what kind of person he was, but by the time she figured it out, she didn't know how to call off the wedding. She was miserable about it."

Suddenly, the two young women came around the corner to face Hope who quickly busied herself with a book on the shelf.

Heather was athletic-looking with long brown hair and hazel eyes ... which narrowed at Hope with suspicion. "Aren't you the cake baker? You did the cake for Carter's wedding."

Hope swallowed. "That's right. You were in the wedding party?"

"I was." Heather took a step closer to Hope. "Do you need help with anything? I'm the assistant librarian. Are you looking for anything in particular?"

"No, no." Hope returned the book to the shelf. "Thanks. I was just looking around. Nice to see you." She wheeled and hurried to the restroom where she splashed her face with water as her mind raced. *Heather said she was glad Randy was dead. She said he got what he deserved. She said Carter didn't want to marry Randy and was miserable about it. Did Heather kill Randy? Did Carter murder him? Did they work together?*

Hope would contact Derrick as soon as she could to report what she'd heard.

As Hope and Cori walked past the church on their way home from the library, they saw the orange construction tape was still in place. Hope looked over and couldn't help but wonder about Randy taking hits from a silver flask at the church. Where exactly had they been drinking? Out of sight, for sure, but where?

"Come on," Hope said. "Let's walk around the church."

"Why?" Cori asked with narrowed eyes. "Don't tell me you're going to investigate the murder."

"I don't investigate."

"Then what do you call it when you start researching an unsolved event?"

"I just want to look around. That's all."

"And what are you looking around for?" Cori questioned.

"Nothing, in particular. I'm just looking."

"You're never just looking. That's like doing an online search. You have to specify something, or else you get nothing."

"Don't argue, just come with me." Hope put her arm around her daughter's shoulders. They walked to the front doors of the church, where they paused for a moment. To Hope, the front door area wasn't a likely place for Randy and Percy and whoever else joined them to stand before the wedding. There would be too many people coming and going and there would be little chance to poison someone at the front of the church.

They walked around the side of the church, past the attached chapel with its own orange-taped door. Hope paused to look around. If she stood close enough to the door, she wouldn't be visible from the street or the parking lot.

Randy and Percy could have stood there and poured down a few ounces before the ceremony.

Is that what they did?

She would have to ask Detective Derrick about that, too.

There was a walkway from the parking lot to a side door which would have been off-limits for the wedding party. Another walkway led to the sacristy, where the pastor would have seen the groom, so that was probably the wrong spot also. The bridesmaids would be at the back of the church, perhaps in the choir loft, along with the bride. It would have been a standard array of people and very little opportunity for poison.

As they reached the sidewalk again, Hope was no

more enlightened than before. She stared at the church and decided that the door to the side chapel was the place where Randy and Percy must have been drinking. Even as Hope watched, a car pulled to the curb.

"Miss Hope," someone called from the car, and Hope was reminded of the Southern habit of adding "Miss" to a first name.

As Hope watched, Carter Remby, the would-be bride, left the vehicle. From the other side, came Percy, the best man.

"I'm glad I caught you," Carter said. "Mother told me about chatting with you in the bakery and I wanted to add my own assurance that no one holds you the least bit responsible. We all know it wasn't the cake or anything else at the reception. I hope you don't believe otherwise."

"I appreciate your kindness, but I wasn't worried about being blamed. I knew what was baked into the cake." After hearing what Heather had said in the library about Carter not wanting to go through with the marriage, Hope eyed the young woman with distrust. "I'm very sorry about what happened to Randy."

"Thank you," Carter told her.

Hope noticed that Percy stood close to Carter

with a kind smile and an adoring expression. He seemed to hover over the young woman like a protective bodyguard. Percy clearly cared for and wanted what was best for Carter. Hope found it almost touching.

After another minute of talk, Carter and Percy climbed into the car and drove away.

"That guy is weird," Cori said as they walked on.

"Weird how?" Hope asked.

"He kept looking at the church, as if he couldn't believe the place was being renovated."

"Maybe, he saw something. A rabbit running over the grass, maybe?"

"Or, he was worried he would be found out as a sinner."

Hope laughed. "Everyone sins, Cori."

"Yeah, but most of us don't look so guilty."

"Like when you do?"

"I never look guilty ... except to you sometimes. Mothers have guilt radar or something."

"Remember that the next time you're tempted to do something wrong. I have guilt radar."

Cori rolled her eyes, and they walked on.

After dinner, Hope took her time cleaning up. She wasn't in any particular hurry to get to her attic office, but she knew she couldn't stay away. She had the feeling that Max was waiting for her, eager for the news of the day. And there was news, just not the kind Max was looking for. When Hope entered her office, she found the sheet of paper on her keyboard.

My dear Mrs. Herring,

Here is a list of the places Captain Jack Thomas liked to frequent. I'm certain the list is woefully inexact and incomplete, as I did not frequent the same refuges for those without purse or prospects. If I remember more, I will provide a second list.

1. *THE SALTY DOG. This tavern of low esteem was on Water Street in Wilmington, close to the wharf. No person of stature would frequent the place, as it was filled with drunken sailors and worse. Captain Thomas was said to be a regular.*

2. *LAMPLIGHTER INN. Also in Wilmington, on Oak Street. Another establishment that served those of lesser means. The Lamplighter was said to be the headquarters of the Black Eight, a loathsome cabal that believed in kidnap for profit. They were slain*

on Christmas Eve by a band of righteous citizens.

3. *THE VELVET GARTER. The less savory incarnation of THE MARITINE CLUB. The Garter as it is, or was, known, provided gambling, alcohol, and women for the likes of Captain Thomas. Thomas was known to cheat at cards and was stabbed once for such behavior. Wilmington on Third Street.*

4. *MRS. TROWBRIDGE'S BOARDING HOUSE. Located on Fifth Street. Captain Thomas would often stay there when in port. Mrs. Trowbridge runs a reputable establishment, but money be money. She took in the bad with the good.*

5. *THE BLOCKADE RUNNER. In New Bern, and it's another tavern with little good to say about it. The Runner, as it is known, was where Captain Thomas picked up Mr. Kendrick (see Charlotte Mae Kendrick) who later jumped ship in Havana, Cuba.*

These are the places and haunts where you are most likely to find information about Captain Thomas. Well, you may run into those whose ancestors had some dealings with the man. I realize that it will take more than a bit of digging to reconstruct the captain's doings in these environs. Yet, I have great faith in you, Mrs. Herring. You strike me as the sort of person who completes any project you choose to take on. Bravo.

Sincerely,

Maximillian Johnson

Hope read the list twice, and she had no doubt that most, if not all, of the places on the list had been overtaken by time and ceased to exist. She had no idea what the average life of a tavern was, but it was generally measured in years, not centuries. Yet, she knew she would try to find these places and discover their histories.

As a teacher and researcher, she knew that often gems were found in the least likely places. She typed the names and addresses into an email, and sent it to Cori. Hope knew her daughter would probably grouse about the extra work, but that couldn't be helped. Hope reasoned that as long as her daughter's new friend, Will, was around, Cori would be okay with doing the research.

She looked around, but Max wasn't there. "Max?"

"Mrs. Herring."

Hope turned to the voice, and there he was. He was exactly the same as before, dressed in his funeral suit.

"I have some news," Hope said.

"For which, I eagerly await."

"Cori was able to trace Mrs. Kendrick today. Did you know she was married at least three times?"

"She was on number two when I was murdered," he said. "But, I don't doubt she buried half a dozen before she moved on."

"If I may ask, whatever happened to her first husband?"

"He stayed in Cuba, as far I know. Claiming he was dead, she remarried right away."

"I thought one had to wait seven years before having someone declared dead."

"Not back in the day," Max said. "In fact, one had merely to move on to the next town and find a willing partner."

"I guess that makes sense. In any case, while we haven't found any clues that she might have killed you, we've established that she did exist."

Max frowned. "You had doubts concerning my truth-telling?"

"I'll be honest with you," Hope said. "I have had my doubts about your *existence*. I've been under a lot of stress lately and I've experienced a number of life changes. I've been wondering if I'm losing my grip on reality."

"I could show myself to your daughter, if that will help."

"No, no, no. Think for a moment what people would do if Cori went around saying this house is haunted, and that she's talked to its ghost."

He nodded. "Very well put. People who claim interaction with the dead are not to be taken seriously. I shall do whatever I can to assure you that I am not part of some dream or vision. In the meantime, I thank you for the update. You did find my list, did you not?"

"You know I did, as I assume you watch, even when you're not visible."

He laughed. "You have found me out, Mrs. Herring. Sometimes, I do watch, but only when you're in here in the office. I take my promises seriously. The bedrooms are strictly off limits. I occasionally roam the rest of the house as the mice show no respect."

Hope laughed. "Mice and insects don't subscribe to human standards. In any case, I'm going to bed. I hope tomorrow is as fruitful as today was."

"I'm sure it will be. Sleep well, Mrs. Herring."

"You, too."

"Thank you. Although I don't really sleep, I do rest. Good night."

Max disappeared, and Hope left her office. She managed to pry Cori from her tablet computer and into bed. As Hope slipped under the covers, she considered the mysteries in her life.

She had the mystery involving her husband's curious accident that occurred under the least likely of circumstances. She had Maximillian's murder, a crime far removed from the present, which made it nearly impossible to solve. She had Randolph's poisoning, which wasn't a murder she was supposed to solve, but her natural curiosity spurred her on. She would like to know how it was done, in which case, she would learn who did it.

If she considered Doug's accident a murder, which she did, there were three murders to solve.

Three mysteries.

No solutions.

With that, she turned over with a sigh, and went to sleep.

There was something about baking that allowed Hope to think even as she created cakes and cupcakes. Yes, she had to pay attention. Yes, she had to create, sometimes standing back and taking a long look before acting. Yet, even though she was involved, her mind could consider other things at times. She could think about the problems at the house. The lawn needed cutting. That wasn't really a problem. It was a scheduling issue, and there was plenty of daylight after work. She could cut it any evening.

The house needed cleaning, and that was another chore that needed nothing but time. She could assign some of that to Cori. Laundry didn't even require daylight. She chided herself for being too lazy to get it done. Hope knew she should keep a list, but that seemed so ... confining. A list was like a task master, something to keep her working hours on end. Who wanted that?

It was too hot to eat lunch outside, so Hope munched on her salad in the diner. The woman who sat down next to Hope looked to be in her mid-sixties. She smiled pleasantly, her black hair dyed, her smile genuine.

"Do you mind if I sit here?" the woman asked.

J. A. WHITING & NELL MCCARTHY

"You're more than welcome." Hope nodded with a friendly smile.

"This is a popular place around lunch time. By the way, I'm Margaret Kinston. And I understand that you're the person who wants to know some things about Castle Park."

22

Hope was a bit surprised, and it must have shown on her face.

"No, I don't read minds," Margaret said with a chuckle. "Harley Story mentioned that you were interested in the history of Castle Park. He described you so well, I couldn't help but recognize you."

"Oh, did he tell you to look for the woman who appears exhausted and anxious?" Hope kidded.

Margaret laughed. "On the contrary, you look relaxed and professional. I'm certain you know how attractive you are."

"Maybe the old me was. The new me, not so much. But I'm happy to meet you. I'm Hope Herring."

As the women shook hands, the waitress

appeared and Margaret ordered her lunch of hamburger and fries.

"I know I'm not supposed to eat like this," Margaret said. "But I just can't help it. The burgers here are wonderful, and who doesn't like fries?"

"I'm with you on that," Hope said. "But I work at the bakery. If I'm not careful, I get more than my share of calories there."

"You're the cake maker. That's right, it was your cake that ... well, let's just say it was an unfortunate event."

"Very unfortunate for the groom."

"Reminds me of Eleanor Rivers. She was jilted on her wedding day, which isn't the same as having the groom drop dead, but, anyway, Eleanor's father went out that night, hunted down the man who jilted his daughter, and shot the man dead. Of course, he was convicted of the killing, but the judge took pity on the father and gave him only two years in prison. And to tell the truth, the dead man's father didn't protest. He said he would have done the same thing. Poor Eleanor, though, never did marry. I guess no one wanted to risk being married with a murdering father-in-law around."

Margaret laughed and Hope joined her.

"Now," Margaret said. "What can I help you with?"

Hope thought a moment. She knew she needed help with the Maximillian Johnson research, but she wasn't sure how much to reveal to Margaret. In a way, Hope thought of the murder as her private quest.

"To tell you the truth," Hope said. "I've been looking into the murder of Maximillian Johnson, the man who built the house I live in."

"That's right. You bought the haunted house. Well, some people say it's haunted. I suppose an unsolved murder is exactly what a mystery solver like you would find interesting."

"Who said I was a mystery solver?"

"Oh, everyone says that. Weren't you sitting with Derrick, the detective, the other day? You must forgive us our little grapevines, but sitting on the courthouse square was bound to start people talking. Of course, your reputation preceded you. I believe it was Jo Ellen Parker, bless her heart, who told everyone that you came from Ohio. And today, with the Internet, looking up someone is so much easier than it used to be."

Hope shook her head. "I'm still amazed at how

easy it is. I never considered myself all that interesting."

"Oh, everyone from another place is interesting. Why, even Sandra Remby said you were the nicest Northerner she's ever met. Of course, not everyone will say the same about Sandra. I'm guessing you probably already know that."

"Sandra was very nice to me," Hope said. "After she found out it wasn't the cake."

Margaret laughed. "That's just like Sandra. So, tell me, who *did* give poor Randolph that dose of poison?"

"I have no idea," Hope said. "Derrick has some suspects, but it's very difficult to figure out."

"Do you know the old saying ... smiling faces tell lies."

"That's true. And just about everyone smiles."

"Oh, yes. So I bet Derrick has his work cut out for him. I know you don't have time right now to go over all the information I have about Maximillian Johnson's murder," Margaret said, "but when you get a day off, give me a call. I'll go over everything I know about it with you. Maybe you can put your skills to work and figure out Maximillian Johnson's murderer."

"That would be great," Hope told the woman and they exchanged contact information.

As the afternoon wore on, Hope thought about the saying "smiling faces tell lies." That made sense. The world was filled with hucksters and frauds and people whose wicked thoughts were hidden behind a pleasant façade. Why did that speak to her? She didn't know for certain. But she did believe in her intuition.

Cori was her usual bubbly self, which meant Will had been at the library. Hope could have kissed Will, since he had single-handedly pushed Cori's sense of loss to the back of the bus. As long as Cori and Will were searching the internet for long-lost people, all would be well. Now, all Hope had to worry about was school. If that went well too....

On their way home, they walked by the church when Hope had an idea. She'd been thinking about Heather and Carter and whether one, or both of them, would want Randy gone so badly that they would resort to murder. Did one of them quietly see Randy before the ceremony and offer him a drink of something? If they did, did they then hide the vial of poison somewhere in the church?

"Do you think we can get inside?" Hope asked Cori.

"Why would you want to get inside?"

"I'd like to look around."

"Didn't the police do that?"

"I suppose they did some looking, but the church has been closed since right after the ceremony. Maybe, they weren't so thorough because the groom died at the country club."

Hope stepped off the sidewalk and headed around the side of the church.

"Shouldn't you ask permission?" Cori said.

"Well, we could, but I think we'll try this first."

"Why?"

"Because everyone knows everything in this town."

"What? That doesn't make any sense. Besides, it's getting dark already."

"Not too dark. And I'm guessing there will be lights on inside."

"*If* we can get inside," Cori said.

"What do you bet there's an unlocked door?"

"Who would leave it unlocked?"

Hope walked around until she came to the chapel door, with its orange tape intact.

"Contractors sometimes leave a door unlocked, although people won't think it's unlocked."

"Because there's tape across it?"

"It would stop most people automatically."

Hope reached across the tape and tried the door. It wasn't locked, and she smiled. But then, it wouldn't open all the way either, since the tape was across the doorframe.

"Now what?" Cori asked.

"As you said, it's getting dark," Hope said and gently pulled off the orange tape.

"I don't think you're supposed to do that." Cori had her hand on her hip.

"It's okay, we'll reattach it when we leave."

"Right."

There were several lights on in the church, but their light was feeble. Hope could see enough to avoid the scaffolding and the paint stained drop cloths, but not nearly enough to conduct a thorough search, but she had an idea and didn't think she'd need a thorough search. She looked around, letting her eyes adjust to the low light.

"This is spooky," Cori said and stepped closer to her mother.

"What are you talking about?" Hope asked with a smile. "You live in a haunted house, and you think this church is spooky?"

"Our house is haunted? I thought you said it wasn't."

"It's not, but everyone thinks it is."

"This place is still spooky."

Hope looked at the door they'd come through and then turned to where the altar stood. Most of the chapel was hidden from the main body of the church which meant someone might be able to hide something and not be seen doing it.

She moved to the small altar in the chapel and studied it for a moment. Above the altar was a cross, and to one side, in the corner was a statue under a drop cloth. Hope moved away from the altar and approached the statue. Although the stained-glass windows let in a little light, Hope was beginning to think that perhaps it was too dark to find anything.

"What are you doing?" Cori asked.

"If you wanted to hide something in this chapel, where would you put it?

"In here? With all the paint stuff? I don't know. The altar maybe, or behind that statue."

"Exactly." Hope leaned and looked around the statue. "I wish I had a flashlight."

"You do," Cori said. She pulled out her phone and started the "torch" app. The bright light made Hope smile.

"I knew there was a reason I brought you," Hope chuckled. She accepted the phone and shone the light behind the statue. Something back there glinted. Encouraged, she reached for the object just as something crashed through a window, making Hope and Cori jump.

"What was...?" Hope didn't finish the question. Fire flashed on one of the drop cloths and flames shot up along the scaffolding.

23

"Mom!" Cori screamed.

Hope started to pull her hand back from behind the statue, but she knew that if she didn't grab the item, it would be lost.

"Mom!" Cori screamed again.

Hope stretched her hand, and her fingers brushed the shiny object. Behind her she heard the loud whoosh as the flames spread to more of the paint-covered drop cloths.

Hope jerked her hand free from the small space behind the statue with such force that she lost her balance and fell onto her back. She inhaled the fumes filling the chapel and coughed as she scrambled to her feet.

The flames were already licking at the ceiling.

She glanced at the door, but it was cut off by a wall of fire.

Cori stood shaking with tears streaming down her cheeks.

"Come on!" Hope grabbed Cori's hand and they ran for the front door. Behind them, smoke and fumes billowed in the chapel.

They reached the front door and pushed.

Nothing happened.

The door was locked. Hope frantically banged the door with her shoulder, but it didn't budge.

"Mom?" Cori shouted over the roar of the flames.

"Don't worry," Hope said and looked around.

There were two other doors, one on either side. Flames and smoke raced toward them. Did they have time to try both doors? Hope couldn't tell, but she didn't have time to work out some sort of strategy. She grabbed Cori's hand.

"This way," Hope yelled.

They choked on the smoke as they ran to the right. Hope prayed that the door would open. The fire was spreading incredibly quickly, fed by the paint and wood. They reached the door and pushed.

Nothing.

Hope didn't hesitate. She spun and dragged Cori in the opposite direction. She cursed the contractor for violating the fire code. Trapped people needed a way out.

The door didn't move.

Hope looked behind. The fire had entered the main section of the church and was still spreading. She knew that the fumes and smoke would probably kill them if they didn't get out soon.

"Pound on the door," Hope shouted to Cori. "And scream."

Hope turned around and squinted through the smoke. There had to be something she could use.

She spotted the baptismal font with the metal cross attached to it, and took aim at the cross. It took a kick with all of her weight behind it, but she managed to snap off the cross.

"Forgive me," she whispered and ran across to where Cori was still hammering the door.

"Step back," Hope said.

There was a stained glass window in the door, and as she hit the glass with the cross, Hope didn't care about anything except getting Cori out alive. It took several hits, but she managed to smash the glass as the hot air from behind rushed past.

"Go now." Hope pulled her daughter closer to the door.

"You won't make it through the window," Cori protested. "It's too small."

"Yes, I will. Just go!"

Hope watched as Cori squeezed through the broken window. It wasn't exactly tight, but then, Cori was much smaller.

Hope ducked as the wooden pews behind her popped and crackled in the flames. Once Cori was out, Hope stuck her arms and head through the window and wiggled with all her might. Although she was partially out, when her hips reached the window frame, she stopped, stuck there.

Cori grabbed Hope's hands and pulled. "Come on, Mom. Squeeze through."

Hope turned her head and saw the black smoke and red flames shooting from the blown out windows along the side of the church. It looked as if an inferno had taken up residence inside.

Cori pulled hard, but it did not good. "Mom," she wailed.

"Turn sideways," a man's voice commanded.

Hope saw Harley Story standing next to Cori.

"Come on, Hope. The widest part is the diagonal," Harley shouted at her. "Turn your hips and we'll pull."

Hope backed off a tad and then turned so her

hips angled through the window. Cori grabbed one hand and Harley grabbed the other.

"On three," Harley said. "We pull, and you push."

"Hurry," Hope cried.

"One, two, three!"

As the two pulled her arms, Hope wiggled, and for a moment, it seemed as if nothing would happen, but then, her right hip wiggled through, and in seconds, she was out through the window.

Harley and Cori pulled Hope to her feet. She immediately felt her back pocket where she'd placed the item she'd fetched from behind the statue in the chapel.

"Let's get out of here." Harley began to run.

Cori and Hope dashed from the church. In the distance, Hope could hear the sirens of the fire trucks and police cars.

They crossed the street and watched as the emergency vehicles arrived. It was clear to Hope that there was no chance to save the church. Flames were now shooting from the roof.

When she reached back and touched her back pocket again, Hope sighed with relief.

"Thank you," Hope gasped to Harley. "You saved my life."

"I was walking home when I heard your

daughter screaming," Harley said. "You're lucky I was working late. Are you okay? You're both bleeding."

Hope looked at her arms. Several small cuts showed where the broken glass had sliced her. Cori had a fewer small cuts on her arms and wrists.

The EMTs arrived and when they took a look at Hope and Cori, they immediately led them off to be treated.

Hope sat next to Cori in the back of the ambulance and held her daughter's hand as the emergency medical techs cleaned and bandaged their cuts.

They watched through the ambulance's windows as the firefighters battled the fire, but there wasn't much that could be done. All they could manage was to contain the blaze and keep it from spreading. In the dark, the flames were spectacular, but it was a sad and depressing sight. The church was gone.

An awful thought popped into Hope's head. Was it suspicious that Harley Story was walking by the church minutes after it went up in flames? A rush of adrenaline raced through Hope's veins.

Did Harley know Randy? Was there bad blood between them? Did Harley kill Randy? Did he set fire to the church? Hope's heart sank at the thought.

No, it couldn't have been Harley. He wouldn't have been drinking with Randy at the church. Hope was pretty sure she knew who killed Randy, and it wasn't Harley Story.

When the last cut was tended to by the EMTS, Cori and Hope exited the ambulance just as Derrick came around the corner.

24

"Are you okay?" Derrick looked from Cori to Hope.

"Just some scrapes and cuts," Hope answered. "We're very lucky. Nothing serious."

"That's good to hear. What were you doing inside the church?"

"We were looking for something," Cori said, wiping some soot from her forehead.

"We found an unlocked door," Hope said. "We went inside to look around in the chapel. That was when someone threw a fire bomb or whatever it was through one of the windows. The paint and drop cloths caught fire in an instant. We had no chance to stop it. We had to find a way out."

"You're lucky to be alive. Why did you want to see the chapel?"

"For this." Hope held out a small flask.

"A flask?" Derrick's eyes went wide.

"I was thinking about the murder, and I knew Randy had to drink the poison before the ceremony, but the flask Percy gave you was untainted. I wondered if there could be a second flask. I guessed that Percy might have given you a different flask than the one he actually gave Randy to drink from. He must have hidden the flask in the chapel, thinking he could retrieve it later, but then the renovation started and he didn't have the chance."

Derrick asked, "Where did you find it?"

"Behind the statue in the chapel. It was well hidden."

Derrick turned his eyes to the blaze. "Percy must have started the fire."

Hope nodded. "He couldn't take the chance that some worker would find the flask. Most of the doors to the church were locked. We found one open, but there was orange tape across it. Percy probably tried to get into the church to retrieve the flask, but he must have thought every door was locked. He must have come up with the idea of starting a fire in order to get rid of the evidence."

Derrick pulled a plastic baggy from his pocket and held it open. Hope dropped in the flask.

"We'll test it," Derrick said. "I'm guessing it will show us how Randy was poisoned."

When Hope pushed at her hair with trembling fingers, Derrick noticed.

"Need a ride home?"

"That would be great," Hope said. "I'm suddenly feeling exhausted and weak."

"Me, too," Cori said, and Hope wrapped her daughter in a hug.

The ride to the house was short and appreciated. The two Herring women limped inside, and Hope was careful to lock the door behind them.

"Shower time," Hope said. "Then, we'll eat some sandwiches or something. We smell like smoke."

"That sounds good to me," Cori said. "Can I shower first or would you like to?"

"You go ahead, hon," Hope said. "I'll start making the sandwiches."

After a hot shower that didn't last nearly long enough, Hope placed the sandwiches, pickles, and chips onto two plates, and then she and Cori ate at the table and talked about the fire.

"That was really awful," Cori said. "I was so scared, but we managed to stay calm."

"We didn't panic. If you don't panic, you can

think, and if you can think, you can find a way out of the predicament."

"Don't run around in circles, screaming and crying?"

"Well, that's a start."

Cori reached over and squeezed her mother's hand. "We did good, Mom."

"We sure did."

After dinner, Hope went to her office for a few minutes. She had barely taken a seat when Max appeared.

"What did you learn today?" Max asked.

"Nothing," Hope answered with a weary voice.

"Nothing? You had all day, and you learned nothing?"

"First, I worked," Hope said. "And when I work, I don't have time to research a hundred-year-old murder. Second, Cori does most of the research at this point, as she's the one who has the time."

"Perhaps, I should chat with her."

"Don't you dare. If you want your murder solved, you will not engage with Cori. Is that clear?"

"I was just trying to move things along." Max winked. "I don't relish remaining here any longer than is necessary."

"Third, Cori and I almost burned to death inside a church."

Max's face took on an expression of horror. "I heard sirens, but I had no idea you were involved. You came through without injury, I trust?"

Hope showed him her arms. "A few cuts, but it could have been much, much worse. So, that's the reason I don't have any information to share. I'm sorry."

Max folded his arms across his chest. "I apologize. I had no idea you were involved in such a dangerous situation."

"It's not something I wish to go through again."

"Did you cause the fire?"

Hope stared at the ghost. "No, we did not cause the fire, and I like to think that the firebomber didn't know we were inside. Otherwise, it could have been murder, and I would have to join you in the nether world. Then we'd need someone else to solve both our murders."

"I think you'd have to haunt the church," Max said. "You can't just jump about willy-nilly."

Hope smiled. "Let's just say we made no progress today. But tomorrow is another day. Maybe, we'll discover something new."

"You did get my list, correct?" Max asked.

"I did, and we'll work on it. Do you have places to add?"

"Not at the moment, but I may come up with something later. You're sure you're not hurt?"

"I'm sure. And if you don't mind, I'll be going to bed now."

"Will you and your daughter be able to work tomorrow?"

"We will, but there's no guarantee that we'll have information to share. Patience, Max, patience."

"I'm sorry you experienced such a terrible thing today. I'm very glad you and your daughter are safe and sound. May you sleep well and dream good dreams."

Before Hope could respond, Max vanished. She stared at the spot where he'd stood, and realized she was becoming very fond of her ghost.

Hope was indeed sore the next day, but beyond that, she felt just fine. She had been worried about her lungs at one point, but not anymore. Hope dropped off Cori at the library and then she walked to the bakery. She'd just stepped around the counter, when Derrick walked through the door.

"Good morning," he said. "Have a minute?"

Hope joined Derrick outside the bakery where they stood on the sidewalk.

The detective smiled. "We don't yet have an analysis of the flask contents," he began. "But we're hopeful. We did take fingerprints. We found Randy's and Percy's and a third set, I assume belonging to you. If you don't mind, I'd like for you to stop by the station during your lunch hour and give us your prints. We'd like to eliminate that third set."

"I'll make a point of it," Hope said with a nod.

"Good. As you might have guessed, I took a ride out to Percy's house last night. He wasn't there. His parents said they didn't know where he was. They said they'd make sure he came to the station this morning, but he hasn't arrived. I called his parents, and they claim they still don't know where Percy is."

"Do you believe them?"

"I do. I sort of hinted that I simply needed to firm up some details about the day of the murder. They have no reason to suspect that Percy is involved in the church fire."

"That's a clever way of handling things."

"Yes, well, that's the bad news. The worse news is that local media is making a big deal of the fire, including the fact that you and your daughter were inside at the time. Have they bothered you yet?"

Hope shook her head.

"They will, and when they do, I would appreciate it if you didn't mention the flask."

"I don't think the media need to know anything about that," Hope said with a grin.

"I'm certain that at some point the insurance people will want to talk to you. I'm guessing they'll accept the firebombing explanation. You're not a pyro, and even an amateur would secure a ready exit before they set a fire."

"Thank you for the vote of confidence."

"You're very welcome," Derrick grinned. "Have a good day and remember to keep quiet about the flask for now."

"What flask?" Hope pretended she knew nothing about what the detective was talking about.

Derrick chuckled and walked away.

Inside the bakery, Edsel eyed Hope. "What did he want?"

"You know the church burned last evening, right?"

Edsel nodded. "I got word of that this morning."

"Well, my daughter and I were inside when it happened."

The woman's eyes went wide. "You set fire to the church?"

Hope shook her head. "No, no, nothing like that. Someone threw a firebomb through a window and the drop cloths and paint went up in flames. We were lucky to escape."

"What were you doing inside the church?"

"Let's just say we were looking for something."

Edsel shook her head. "In that case, don't tell me. People think I know something about something, and they come in to haunt me. I'm better off not knowing."

At that moment, a pretty, young woman with a notebook entered, followed by a cameraman toting a handheld camera.

"Good morning," the woman said. "I'm from WNCT news, and I'd like to ask a few questions, if you don't mind."

"I don't know anything," Edsel said. "Absolutely nothing."

"All right," Hope said. "But let's do this outside. Is that okay?"

The woman nodded. "That would be fine."

Before Hope stepped outside, she texted Cori.

DO NOT TALK TO REPORTERS!!!

Much to Hope's chagrin, she spent the morning

with journalists. Several newspaper reporters showed up, as well as more local film crews. They all asked the same questions, and Hope gave the same answers. She was careful not to divulge anything about the flask or even Cori for that matter. When someone asked about Cori, Hope deflected the question, but she didn't lie. She had to admit that Cori was there.

What were they doing there?

They thought they heard a dog inside. Unfortunately, that *was* a lie.

Hope didn't go out for lunch, but instead worked on the cakes she hadn't yet produced. She left Edsel to hold off anyone who wanted to talk about the fire —or anything else. And Edsel proved more than capable.

25

Hope worked through the afternoon and by quitting time, she'd caught up with her baking, and the media people had moved on. She was thankful for the short news cycle.

At that point, she remembered that she was supposed to have her fingerprints taken. She sent an apology to Derrick and promised to do it the next morning. He was fine with her message. She trudged to the library, feeling worn out and slow.

Cori wasn't waiting, which surprised Hope. Ordinarily, Cori was more than ready to leave.

Where are you? Hope texted.

At home. Cori texted back.

What are you doing there?

Waiting for you.

Be right there.

Hope frowned and started for home. Cori was supposed to wait for her, but there were several reasons why Cori might have headed home early. She might not have been feeling well, and that certainly made sense after the evening they'd had. The cuts on her arms might be bothering her, or, maybe the media hounds had found her. Since she wasn't supposed to talk to them, she made the decision to go home. It was easier to ignore them from the safety of her bedroom.

Hope wished her daughter had the foresight to avoid the reporters. Still, she needed to impress on Cori the need to use a text or a phone call to alert her mother to a change of plans.

Hope found Cori in her bedroom sitting on the bed, leaning back against the pillows. She looked pale.

"One question," Hope said. "Why did you come home early, and why didn't you tell me?"

"That's two questions," a man's voice said.

With her heart racing, Hope whirled towards the voice.

Percy smiled back at her, and he was holding a pistol.

"She didn't call you because she didn't have her phone. I have it." Percy held up Cori's phone.

"What do you want?" Hope couldn't keep the rage from her tone.

"Did you find it?" he asked. "I asked your daughter, but she played stupid. She said you didn't find anything."

"What do you think we might have found?" Hope asked.

"That answer doesn't explain what you were doing inside the church." Percy sneered.

"The church you firebombed?" Hope's face was red.

"I didn't firebomb anything."

"Oh, yes, you did," Hope said. "And it probably won't be very hard to prove."

Percy took a step towards Hope. "What were you doing there?"

"We thought we heard a dog barking inside and we wanted to let it out."

"Bull. You were looking for something so don't play games with me."

Hope considered for a moment. "You're right, we were looking for something ... and we found it. We found the flask you hid in the chapel."

"I knew it. I knew it," Percy growled. "I should have firebombed that place earlier."

"Why didn't you?" Hope asked trying to buy some time.

"I've been busy helping Carter. I couldn't very well do it when she was with me."

"The police have the flask, and by this time, they've tested it for the poison you used. They're looking for you, Percy. Do yourself a favor and turn yourself in."

"I'm a killer. I murdered my friend. And now I have to murder you."

"You have no reason to harm us," Hope said. "The police already have the flask. It will only make things worse for you."

"I'm already dead," he said. "I'm looking at life in prison. And even if I manage to get a lesser sentence, I'll never be able to be with Carter." Percy's eyes bugged. "I have no reason not to harm you. I have to kill you for what you've done to me."

Hope tried to keep her voice calm and even. "Your family has money. They can hire a clever attorney or two who will work like the devil to keep you out of prison. It might work. Oh, you'll probably have to do some time, but maybe not. The lawyers will have you plead temporary insanity and you might walk."

Percy chuckled. "Two flasks, killing my friend, firebombing the church. I doubt anyone will fall for temporary insanity."

"When we moved into this house," Hope said. "We didn't know that there had been a murder committed here. The first owner of this house, Maximillian Johnson, was killed in the kitchen."

Percy looked confused. "What are you talking about?"

"Mr. Johnson's murder is still unsolved, but think what might have happened had he seen his killer? Maybe, just maybe, he might have managed to pick up something to use as a weapon and at least have a fair fight."

"What are you talking about? That old murder means nothing to me."

Hope glanced at Cori whose face was filled with fear and doubt.

"I've been thinking about it," Hope said. "If Max could have grabbed something, like that picture frame on Cori's dresser, he might have managed to hit the killer in the head or something."

"That picture frame can't help you," Percy said.

"If anyone has a case for temporary insanity, it's you."

"You're not listening," Hope said. "Max was all alone, but he could have done something, if he'd only seen his attacker. He would have been in a position to fight back."

"Enough about Max whoever. Move closer to your daughter." Percy waved the pistol.

"Max has to go first," Hope said.

"You're crazy." Percy snarled and turned to Cori. "Who first? You or your crazy mother?"

"Me," Hope said. "Let Cori go."

"You, it is." Percy turned, aiming the gun at Hope.

That was when the picture frame flew across the room and hit Percy right between the eyes.

26

Percy collapsed, and Hope jumped forward. She ripped the pistol from the dazed man's hand and stepped back.

"Call 911." Hope handed her own phone to her daughter before wrapping Cori in a hug.

"How did you do that?" Cori asked.

"I didn't do anything, hon. Call 911."

Hope held the pistol on Percy for the ten minutes it took for the police to arrive. They were quick to disarm her and handcuff Percy.

Hope took Cori to the kitchen where they waited for Derrick. The EMTs who had treated Hope and Cori the night before showed up and hovered over them until they were certain that neither one had been harmed. They'd no sooner walked out when Derrick walked in.

"You're all right?" Derrick asked with a worried expression.

"We're just shaky," Hope said. "This is the second night in a row that we faced a deadly problem."

"You've managed to stay alive both times. Tell me what happened with Percy."

Cori and her mother told the story, and when Hope reached the point where the picture frame flew across the room, she hesitated.

"Percy was so busy with Cori," Hope said, keeping eye contact with her daughter, "that I had the chance to grab the picture frame. I managed to throw it into Percy's face, and it dazed him. That was when I grabbed his gun."

"That was one heck of a brave thing to do," Derrick said. "I suppose you had no choice."

"Percy admitted to killing Randy and fire-bombing the chapel," Hope said. "He was about to kill us. I wasn't going to let him hurt my daughter so I took the chance."

"That right?" Derrick asked Cori.

"Yes," Cori said. "It happened just like Mom said."

The interview lasted a few more minutes, but Derrick didn't press.

"Don't bother coming in for fingerprinting," Derrick said to Hope. "I think we have enough to send Percy away for a long time. By the way, did he say why he killed Randy?"

Hope shook her head. "Not really. I suppose it was a mixture of envy and unrequited love. He'd dated Carter in high school, and when she left him in favor of Randy, Percy must have lost his mind with jealousy. He probably thought that with Randy gone, Carter would come back to him."

"It's funny how many people think that way. Get rid of the competition, and you move up the ladder. It doesn't usually work out that way."

Hope said, "Percy firebombed the church in order to get rid of the second flask, but I don't think he knew we were inside when he did it."

"Doesn't matter. He murdered Randy."

It was another hour before the hubbub quieted, and Hope was alone with Cori. She heaped ice cream into two bowls and joined her daughter at the table.

"Can you do it again?" Cori asked, as she spooned ice cream into her mouth.

"Do what again?"

"Make something move."

"I can't make anything move. I threw the picture frame," Hope said.

"Did you?" Cori tilted her head to the side with an expression of disbelief. "I didn't see you do that and since the frame was a couple of steps away from you, I'd say you couldn't possibly have thrown it."

"Then, what do you think happened?" Hope asked.

"Magic," Cori said. "You must know magic. You can make things move just by thinking it or wiggling your nose or saying some spell or something. Like a Harry Potter book, you can work magic, but you can't show it to anyone."

Hope couldn't keep from chuckling as she shook her head. "Afraid not, hon, although that would be awesome. There were no spells, no magic, nothing, but a desperate need for something to happen."

"I don't understand. What are you saying?"

"The human brain is a wonderful organ, and its powers are largely unknown and unexplored. I've read that there are people who supposedly can make objects move just by using their brain power, but that's not me. If you do some research on brain power, you'll find people who lifted cars when they needed to."

"Lifted cars?"

"There are reports of people who moved cars in order to save a loved one. Somehow, the mind finds a way to provide extra power to a person's muscles. Things that a person could never do under normal circumstances can be done if the need arises."

"So, you're saying that because there was a need—"

"A desperate need."

"Because there was a desperate need, you were able to make the picture frame fly across the room and hit Percy in the face?"

"That's the only explanation I can come up with," Hope said with a shrug. "It's not something I can do any time I want. I mean, let's face it, if I could make objects move, I wouldn't carry the dishes to the cabinets."

Cori laughed. "Yeah, that sort of thing would come in handy, wouldn't it?"

"But don't underestimate your brain," Hope said. "Sometimes, when you least expect it, your brain will come up with some amazing thought or power."

"I'll remember not to give you a reason to toss a picture frame at me."

Hope smiled at her daughter. "Well, if you do

your homework and your chores, then I don't think you'll have to worry about any picture frames."

"Good to know," Cori grinned.

After thirty minutes of conversation, Hope asked, "When you were at the library today, did you manage to find any new information on the people or places on our lists?"

"Not today. I was busy telling Will about the church fire. Then, when I went to lunch and Will couldn't go, Percy came around the corner and took me. I was scared, but I was really angry, too."

"You're a strong, brave person. You've been through a lot over the past months."

"Yeah," Cori said softly. "We need to keep moving forward. We can't let anything stop us."

Hope's throat tightened. She gave her daughter a nod.

"So, no, I didn't learn anything today, but tomorrow, I'll be back at it."

"Me, too."

Hope and Cori talked while they ate their ice cream, and Hope was pleased that Cori bought into the explanation of how the picture frame had moved. In fact, after a while, Hope wasn't so sure it wasn't the correct answer.

"You know," Hope said, "ice cream for dinner can't happen every night."

"I know," Cori said. "But it sure tasted good."

"Do you want to sleep in my bed tonight?" Hope asked.

"No, I think I'll be all right. I was scared. It was a big gun." Cori looked at her mother. "Would you like me to sleep in your bed with you? Are you okay?"

"I was very afraid, but I think I'll be okay. Thanks for offering though."

Before Hope went up to her office in the attic, she made sure Cori was safe and warm in her bed.

As Hope climbed the stairs, she managed a smile. Despite odds to the contrary, she and Cori had managed to survive the fire and the kidnapping. She was more than thankful for that.

"Max," Hope said as soon as she sat at her workstation.

"Good evening, Mrs. Herring."

Hope turned to see Max smiling back at her.

"Thank you for helping us," Hope said. "It was you, wasn't it?"

"Indeed, it was," he said. "That ruffian had no call to hold you and your daughter at gunpoint."

"He did not, but you did take your time. I thought, perhaps, you weren't going to help."

"As I recall, madam, you expressly forbade me to enter the bedrooms. I was merely following instructions."

"Well, let's add an addendum to the instructions. If you pass by, and you hear voices, please listen for a second or two. If we're in trouble, you are free to enter and help. How's that?"

"I can live with that, if you can."

"I can. And, Max, I can't thank you enough. That young man was going to kill us."

"I thought as much. You're most welcome. I will act any time I am needed."

"I'm sorry we haven't done much on your case. We had the church fire last night, and today, it was non-stop questions from all over. So, we haven't had the chance to do anything on your murder. I'm sorry, but we haven't given up."

"I have waited a century. What's another month, or two or three? I'm glad to hear that you're still up for the job."

"We are. Cori and I will continue to pursue every lead we can find."

"Thank you, Mrs. Herring. Now, I recommend sleep."

"That's where I'm headed. I'm exhausted."

Hope stood, and they faced each other.

"Call me Hope. Good night, Max."

"Good night, Hope."

Max faded from view, and she walked down to her bedroom feeling strangely happy.

The next morning, Hope was busy with a cake, when Edsel interrupted.

"You have some folks who want to say hello," Edsel said.

"I'm really busy," Hope said, thinking they must be reporters. "Can they come back?"

"I don't think so."

"Okay, I'll be right out."

Hope was wiping her hands on a towel when she walked out to the counter where Sandra stood with another woman.

"Mrs. Herring," Sandra said. "I want you to meet Dolly Windom. Dolly is Randolph's mother."

Hope stepped up and offered her hand. "I'm so very sorry for your loss, Mrs. Windom."

"Thank you," Dolly said. "I came because I wanted to thank you personally for how you solved my Randolph's murder. Words cannot express my sincere gratitude."

"You're very welcome," Hope said. "But I only did what I could do. The police are the ones who need to be thanked."

"And they will be. I'm planning a special memorial service for Randolph, and I would appreciate it if you would not only bake some desserts for the occasion, but join us in the celebration of Randolph's life."

"I'd be more than happy to," Hope said. "May I bring my daughter?"

"Of course. Nothing would make me happier."

After a few more minutes of chat, Sandra and Dolly left, and Edsel clapped her hands.

"You're in for it now," Edsel said with a grin.

"Why do you say that?" Hope asked.

"Never trust the Windoms. Don't get close to that bunch."

Hope laughed. "You're kidding."

"I'm not kidding. Keep your distance from them. That family is a bunch of black widows, child, a bunch of black widows. But don't you worry. You're not alone here. You've got friends now ... me, Derrick, and Harley Story. We'll watch out for you, don't you worry."

Hope felt warmth spread through her chest. "Thanks."

Returning to work on the cake, Hope raised an eyebrow. Were there Windoms in town around the time when Maximillian was murdered? Maybe that was something she should look into when she got home and could do some internet sleuthing.

Hope smiled.

She was beginning to like Castle Park a whole lot more than she ever thought she was going to.

———————

I hope you enjoyed *Silver Linings*! The next book in the series, *Blood Moon*, can be found here:

viewbook.at/BloodMoonHopeHerring

THANK YOU FOR READING!

Books by J.A. WHITING can be found here:
www.amazon.com/author/jawhiting

To hear about new books and book sales, please sign up for our mailing list at:
www.jawhiting.com

Your email will never be sold, shared, or spammed.

If you enjoyed the book, please consider leaving a review. A few words are all that's needed. It would be very much appreciated.

BOOKS BY J. A. WHITING

OLIVIA MILLER MYSTERIES (not cozy)

SWEET COVE PARANORMAL COZY MYSTERIES

LIN COFFIN PARANORMAL COZY MYSTERIES

CLAIRE ROLLINS COZY MYSTERIES

PAXTON PARK PARANORMAL COZY MYSTERIES

SEEING COLORS PARANORMAL COZY MYSTERIES

ELLA DANIELS WITCH COZY MYSTERIES

SWEET BEGINNINGS BOX SETS

SWEET ROMANCES by JENA WINTER

BOOKS BY J.A. WHITING & ARIEL SLICK

GOOD HARBOR WITCHES PARANORMAL COZY
MYSTERIES

BOOKS BY J.A. WHITING & AMANDA DIAMOND

PEACHTREE POINT COZY MYSTERIES

DIGGING UP SECRETS PARANORMAL COZY
MYSTERIES

BOOKS BY J.A. WHITING & MAY STENMARK

MAGICAL SLEUTH PARANORMAL WOMEN'S FICTION COZY MYSTERIES

VISIT US

www.jawhiting.com

www.bookbub.com/authors/j-a-whiting

www.amazon.com/author/jawhiting

www.facebook.com/jawhitingauthor

www.bingebooks.com/author/ja-whiting

J. A. WHITING BOOKS